"I'll see　　　　　　　　　　　　　　　e."

Holly ra　　　　　　　　　　　　　　hall back into her　　　　　　　　　　running into her room and flopping onto the messy bed.

This was crazy. One neighbor was missing, and another might be involved. How many times had she looked into his bedroom, listened to him play the same sad tune on the same piano, and she had never suspected a thing? He looked normal, not pale, not gaunt with stringy hair. Nothing how a villain would look like in a movie.

Her fears melted into the back of her mind as different thoughts took center stage, thoughts about Luke and his shirt-lessness.

The Man Across the Alley

by

Emilie Barage

Murder For Your Thoughts Series

The Man Across the Alley

Cover Art by *Diana Carlile*

The Wild Rose Press, Inc.
PO Box 708
Adams Basin, NY 14410-0708
Visit us at www.thewildrosepress.com

Publishing History
First Edition, 2022
Trade Paperback ISBN 978-1-5092-4076-0
Digital ISBN 978-1-5092-4077-7

Published in the United States of America

Dedication

I want to thank all the ladies who helped me realize I can survive a lot of things, especially heartbreak: Nikki, Sean, Jessica, Kim, Meghan, Lindsey, Caroline, Diana, Julie, Taylor, Katherine and so many more.

I want to thank my mom for letting me steal her romance novels and for being the absolute best.

Finally, I want to thank Karen and Georgia, who inspire me to stay sexy and not get murdered all day, every day.

Chapter One

"Good God, can't a woman sleep in anymore?"

Holly Harrison dragged a pillow across her head to drown out the incredibly loud noises coming from across the hall. She turned over to look at her phone, the bright screen advised her it was just past eight in the morning. "You've got to be kidding me."

There was no way she was getting back to sleep and boy, she could've used it. After the week she'd had of fitful nights, it seemed as though dark circles were now permanently tattooed under her eyes. She could not stop thinking about her now ex, Nick Bunch. Though she'd only been in a couple of serious relationships throughout her twenty-eight years, she had learned the telltale signs of a forthcoming breakup. When Nick came over and ended things, it hadn't hurt any less.

Grumbling as she got out of bed, Holly walked to the door, stopping to look at her reflection in the mirror on the back. Her brown curls were mussed up in the front of her head and completely flat on the back. Her blue eyes looked sunken thanks to the dark circles living under them. Thanks to frequent walks during sunny weather, freckles now appeared on her olive skin.

With a sigh, she opened the door to the living room to see her roommate, Kate, sitting on the brown-leather couch. Coffee in hand, laptop in lap, she looked every bit the social media model. Her blonde hair spilled out of a messy bun, her tortoiseshell glasses posed perfectly on top of her head and she wore a loose black T-shirt with jean shorts. She was effortlessly pretty—in direct opposition to Holly's dark curly hair, freckled nose, and frumpy clothes. If Kate was the model, Holly was her photographer, never the one in the spotlight.

Kate looked up and smiled. "Well good morning, I wasn't expecting to see you for at least another hour."

Holly looked at her as the crashing and banging erupted right outside their apartment door. "I'm sorry, did you not hear our new neighbors moving in? It sounds like they're wearing shoes made of metal." She winced as another loud bang vibrated through the walls.

"Oh, jeez I didn't really," Kate admitted. "I got so wrapped up in emails."

When the pandemic hit and Chicago mandated a strict stay-at-home quarantine, the pair had worked from home. Now the world was almost back to normal, and the masses did not have to work from home. Restaurants were slowly opening back up and only those who were sick or immune compromised wore masks. Loyal fans returned to their favorite sporting events again, and concert venues were at full capacity.

The roommates, however, stayed put. Kate's managers realized how much money they saved by not maintaining an office while the theater where Holly worked as an assistant to the manager was on the very slow path to reopening, keeping both women at home for the time being. It was not a great time to be working at a small, neighborhood theater. She kept reminding herself that it was only a matter of time until normal life resumed but still found herself missing her tiny office, the phone arguments with bill collectors and haggling with vendors. She missed interacting with the geriatric volunteers who showed patrons to their seats, fending off romantic advances from the college kids who worked the ticket booths.

She missed having something to distract her from...well, being dumped.

While Holly's work assignments became fewer and farther in between, Kate's work flow was the exact opposite. Being a higher up at a marketing agency, her work life had become more hectic as time went on. From the moment she was logged on, there was no slowing down. At night, after she finally logged off the computer, she didn't stop. An avid yoga practitioner, Kate often tried to rope Holly into joining her. If she wasn't doing yoga, she was virtually catching up with friends or family or trying out a new baking recipe. It was her way of coping with the world and Holly would not stop her from keeping herself busy, especially if it meant reaping the benefits of the freshly baked bread her roommate was currently obsessed with making.

Holly shuffled past the couch and into the kitchen to pour herself some coffee. "You're lucky. It's all I'm able to hear." She stared at the dark liquid in her mug, missing her usual coffee shop and the *café americanos* she used to buy. She chuckled as she found herself reminiscing about her morning commute, taking the Brown Line into the Loop, getting off at the State/Lake stop, seeing all the glittering lights of the theaters. If someone told her that she would find herself missing the packed train car and the sometimes-terrible smells that came along with it, she would've laughed in their face.

Looking up from her cup, she glanced out the window to the back porch that they shared with the 'new' noisy neighbor. Would she be able see those responsible for waking her up at such an ungodly hour? Turning, she saw a white T-shirt clad back and a tight pair of buttocks covered in denim jeans come into view—and immediately captured her full attention. She caught a glimpse of dark, curly hair and toned arms as he backed up a step, then moved forward. Whomever belonged to this shirt and jeans combo was dragging something heavy into their kitchen and seemed to have gotten it wedged which meant he had to wiggle several interesting body parts in order to get it out.

Holly didn't mind, she could watch "Jeans Guy" wiggle all day…

"Um, hello?" Kate waved a hand in front of her face. "I said did you need me to make another batch of coffee to help you wake up, but it looks like something has already awakened your…ahem…senses."

At Holly's dirty look, Kate grinned and refilled her cup. "If his face looks as good as his backside, maybe you'll forgive him for making so much noise. Plus, maybe it's time for you to start looking again."

When she turned and walked back into the living room, Holly was there, hot on her heels. "Oh, shut up. I have no desire to look at anyone's face right now." She started shuffling back into her bedroom and called over her shoulder, "And besides, I bet he's moving in with a girlfriend or wife or something."

"Nope. Two guys."

She stuck her head back into the living room. "How do you know that?"

Kate tore her eyes away from her screen and gave her a matter of fact look. "I ran into the super yesterday. He told me it was two guy roomates, moving in together."

Holly narrowed her eyes. "I still don't care what his face looks like."

Shutting her bedroom door, she sat on her bed and stared into space. She did not care if a man moved next door who happened to sport a perfect jeans-clad backside. She had more important things to do, like catch up on this morning's blog posting. Moving to her desk, she sat down and opened her ancient laptop, then stared out the window while she waited for it to boot up.

Murder for Your Thoughts was her favorite true crime blog. It had always been her guilty pleasure—listening to the podcasts, reading the updates on cold cases. *MfYT* was the perfect mix of emotional and humorous intrigue. The writer, known only by the initials R.J., focused on cases occurring in certain regions of the US. For the past week, Chicago took the hot spot. At first, the stories were the most infamous: H.H. Holmes, John Wayne Gacy, and the St. Valentine's Day Massacre from back in the days of Prohibition.

But now, R.J. wrote about more recent cases, ones Holly never heard of. Like the man in Rogers Park who shot two people on the street in broad daylight. Or the one about a lady who set her family's house on fire in Wicker Park to stop domestic abuse. Holly felt both fascinated and terrified reading about these current crimes that were so close to her home.

Opening the browser window, she scanned for the headline for today's posting and sat up straight when she finally found it. *Never Found: The Missing Ladies of Lakeview.*

Lakeview. Her neighborhood. Holly involuntarily looked out her window facing the street. Any one of these people, walking their dogs, on their way to their cars could be taken. They could be the one taking the missing women. With a shake of her head, she pushed the cup of coffee to the other side of her desk. Too much caffeine and being awake this early were messing with her head.

She read on:

One minute she is walking into her apartment after a long day at work, the next she is gone. The story of Ashley Mitchell is similar to that of Courtney Keller, Abby Sosa, and Sam Keffe. The last anyone saw of each of them was when they went into their apartments. Their homes, where they felt safe, where they SHOULD be safe, were the scenes of the crimes. It did not matter that they were all different ethnicities, different ages, or held different jobs. The only connection between any of them was the neighborhood they all lived in.

The police don't seem to have any leads at the moment but of course, that doesn't deter us armchair detectives from looking for the girls, and the truth.

Witnesses report nothing out of the ordinary. No one suspicious looking has been seen, no one caught lurking. Maybe it's the Midwestern friendliness or maybe during these times, everyone is too wrapped up in their own wellbeing to remember to look and listen...

The blog post was long, but Holly devoured every word. By the end of the piece, R.J. had mentioned street names where each of the women lived, not the exact addresses out of privacy. They all lived right around Holly. Each street connected, making a large circle, and her apartment was right in the middle.

Finishing the article, Holly sat and stared out the window again. *How scary,* she thought, *It could've been me.* She let her eyes wander from the window and around her room. With more time spent at home, she'd finally taken the time to create a calm and productive environment. All her furniture was grey with pops of soft green placed throughout the room. Her gaze moved from her bedspread up to her wall, covered in artwork from various shows she had worked on and photos from the ones she had been in. Along with creating a calm space, she had finally taken the time to frame everything and make her room feel a bit more mature.

She turned her head, and her lips turned into a frown as her eyes settled on dried flowers propped up in a glass. Nick had bought her those flowers when she had told him she needed plants to make her space look more grown up. Her mind wandered and she thought about him being in this room, the fun times they had… She quickly shook the memories from her head and turned her attention back to her laptop.

Needing a distraction from the chills running up her spine from the post, she logged onto her work email. Three new posts sat in her inbox. With a sigh of thanks, her thoughts went elsewhere.

Chapter Two

Standing in the middle of his new apartment, Luke Morris put his sweaty hands on his hips and let out a breath of relief. "Well at least everything is in one place now." He turned and saw his roommate splayed across the couch, an arm thrown over his head, moaning, "I hate moving."

Tommy Clanahan's five-foot-ten-inch frame took up about half the couch. He pushed his thick blond hair off his forehead with a sweat band and opted for an 80's look when it came to moving day attire complete with a thin, sweat-soaked tank top and teal running shorts, accentuating what he self-proclaimed as his 'hard worked dad-bod'. When he had answered the door, Luke just chuckled—leave it to Tommy to try and have fun even when moving.

Luke plopped onto the cushion beside him. "Everyone does, and it's usually not this miserable. People tend to start moving at normal hours like eleven rather than eight. How did you even find a company that does it that early?"

"It was cheaper. I've learned my mistake."

"It may have been cheaper, but it probably cost us brownie points with the rest of the building. No one wants to hear a couch being dropped three separate times this early in the morning."

"I'll pay for the scratch in the wall with the money

we saved," Tommy moaned and closed his eyes again.

Luke chuckled and got up. "I'm going to sit on the back porch and hopefully dry off, maybe have a drink. Want one?"

Eyes still closed, Tommy muttered, "Can't. Move."

Luke was not surprised. Having moved in and out of quite a few apartments since college, he had learned to downsize and retain only what was necessary. Tommy, on the other hand, owned every kitchen item, bathroom accessory, and entertainment device known to man, with numerous boxes to prove it. It had been a while since he was able to cook a decent meal for himself, and now all the tools were at his fingertips.

A lot of things were going to be different now. While his job as a web site developer had not been hurt by the pandemic with everyone transitioning to work from home, he could not say the same for his roommate. A local performer before the pandemic closed most public venues, his sources of income had dried up and his ability to pay for his own space went with it.

As things began to open back up, Tommy and the other million performance artists all vied for the same theater slots—and right now luck did not seem to be on his side. It hurt to see his friend, practically a brother to him, struggle in this way, and he wanted to help if he could. Of course, having someone around would probably help him with his own loneliness and solitude, something which he once found comforting.

Working from home was something Luke had done for as long as he had held this job. No terrible commute, no mundane talk with co-workers, no forced happy hours. He considered himself content, but circumstances started to change as the world around him did. The anxiety over the possibility of getting sick, of not knowing if the economy would recover—if it ever did—wondering if his friends were okay, it all built up. When Tommy needed help, Luke jumped at the chance.

He walked into the kitchen and opened the refrigerator door, only to find it empty except for a few random condiments and a case of beer. The clock on the microwave told him it was noon, and he decided it was an appropriate time for the first beer of the day. Grabbing one, he turned to open the screen door to the back porch, stopping in his tracks.

A woman, engrossed in her laptop, sat on one of the patio chairs. The back of the chair tilted against the wall, and she sat with her legs crossed, the computer balanced on her thighs. Eyes never leaving the screen, she reached and grabbed her cup of coffee, took a sip, and carefully placed it back down again.

Luke didn't think she had noticed him yet, standing a few feet away, so he continued to take her in. Her dark brown hair was pulled up into a bun on top of her head, giving the impression she just wanted to get it out of her face, not caring how it looked. Her face, with its intense expression, was cute. An early summer tan brought out the freckles on her nose. Looking farther down her body, he saw she wore a thin, tank top that was pulled down in the front by the weight of her laptop, exposing a low cut, black workout bra. He found himself thinking that it wasn't a bad view. When was the last time he had thought about what was down the front of a woman's shirt? Maybe now with the move, he could make a fresh start, not revert to his isolating tendencies and, against all odds, meet someone new?

Of course, he thought, *maybe I shouldn't just be*

standing and staring at someone. Wouldn't want to be known as the creepy guy in the building.

He opened the door with a loud squeak and made the woman jump in her seat, startled.

Her surprised eyes quickly slid over his body, seeming to linger around his waist for a moment longer, before coming back up to his face. "Hi, you're the new neighbor." She said it as a statement and not a question.

"Uh yeah, hi. I'm Luke. I just moved in today with my friend Tommy."

Her eyebrow raised. "Yeah, I heard. I'm pretty sure the whole building heard." She turned her head back to her screen.

Just as he suspected, their early morning move had made a not-so-great impression with the neighbors. "Yeah, I'm sorry about that. Apparently, it's a cheaper rate to move earlier in the day…" He trailed off, embarrassed. "I promise we'll be quieter when we're out here though. I assume you're the person we share the porch with and not some random lady who broke in so she could sit back here."

When a small smile crept onto her face, he felt pleased.

"No, no, I live here with my friend Kate." She looked back at Luke, grinning. "My name is Holly. Sorry, I didn't mean to come off as…the coffee hasn't kicked in yet." She nodded at the bottle in his hand. "Maybe I should switch to one of those."

"Hey, I'm a firm believer that a drink on your lunch break is necessary, especially when working from home. I'm sorry for disrupting you, by the way."

"I'm not working right now. I'm practically done for the day. I'm just catching up on some reading."

"Oh? News?"

Embarrassed, she turned and looked out over the balcony. "Kind of…it's about crimes happening around the neighborhood. This blog I read, called *Murder for Your Thoughts,* has a round of stories that have happened around here. It's fascinating, and some are still unsolved like these missing girls and I'm just wanting to know more so…" She turned and looked back at him, a sheepish look on her face, "I'm sorry, you did not need all that information."

"No, no, that's actually super interesting. I've never been into true crime before, but I've always loved a good detective movie."

He moved closer and leaned over to look at her screen. Up close, her skin looked velvety soft, and he thought about how nice it would feel to run his hand up and down her arm. He smelled the grapefruit scent of her shampoo. A warm breeze blew toward him, making the scent stronger while reminding him that he needed a shower. He quickly stepped back.

"Sorry, I probably shouldn't stand so close, moving day and all. Um, I should go and unpack the bathroom so I can properly clean up." He walked back inside and turned, speaking through the screen door, "I'll see you around, Holly."

She smiled. "Yeah, you, too."

****

Holly watched as he walked out of her line of sight and waited until she heard the faint sound of a door being closed, hopefully the bathroom door in his apartment. She closed her laptop and took a deep breath, closing her eyes. "Jeans Guy" had a name: Luke.

She should not have been caught off guard. After all,

they shared a porch together, so she was bound to run into him at some point. She just had not expected him to be so…to look so…hot.

He looked to be about six feet tall so he would tower over her even if she had not been sitting, that was for sure. He clearly worked out but wasn't a beefy gym rat. From the look of his forearms, he lifted weights every now and then. When she gave him the quick once-over, she naturally hovered around his butt, wanting to make sure it was the same guy who she saw that morning. She was then drawn to his eyes, they were the most beautiful, seemingly good natured, green eyes that were simply captivating, framed by scruffy beard and messy, curly brown hair. He looked like a guy who would be cast in a Hallmark Channel movie as a small-town farmer who doesn't know how good looking he is. She thought as he came closer to her that his obviously sweaty smell would counteract the beauty before her but, of course, she found herself not hating being near his natural musk.

She opened her eyes, shot up out of her seat, and stretched while looking across the alleyway opposite her porch. Separating her building from the one next door, the space was so narrow that the wooden back stairs and fire escapes jutted out far enough so that they touched. She could see into the bedrooms of three different apartments, two next to each other, and one the next floor up. Although she never formally met the tenants of the building, they had lived there as long as she had, and she felt as if she knew them. That's how it was in this neighborhood, you always saw the same people, walking the same dogs, carrying groceries in each day. You got to know them by sight if not by name.

On the first floor lived two roommates, girls who

looked to be around her own age, Holly saw them usually leaving together in a taxi on Saturday nights. Before quarantine, the girls would leave to go on a night out at the same time as Holly. She remembered walking with them to the train quite a few times, excitedly talking about their plans to each other.

The second apartment on the same floor housed a solitary man who loved to play the piano. He often left his window open and could be heard playing. On a few occasions, Holly had yelled across the alleyway that she liked the song, making him smile. He seemed nice enough but other than those compliments and a few polite exchanges on the street, she didn't really know him well. The apartment above was home to a couple who were expecting a baby. They were pleasant when you passed them on the street and seemed to Holly the perfect couple. She very much enjoyed observing the love they felt for each other.

Seeing the familiar sight of her neighbors, living their lives, doing their daily routines, used to comfort Holly. Now, looking down at her closed laptop, she remembered that not even this pocket of normalcy would remain untouched by the outside world for long.

Chapter Three

Over the next few days, Holly began to put more thought into her appearance. Her normal work-from-home wardrobe up until this point had consisted of various pairs of exercise leggings and tank tops. Since the quarantine fifteen had not bypassed her, she took the time to dig out her stretchy jeans as well as some cute T-shirts and tank tops.

She usually put a tiny bit of effort into her appearance for those rare occasions when she left the house. Now, it seemed every time she opened the door, Luke was there, grabbing a package, going to the mailbox, or running to the corner shop. They always had the same exchange: he'd said hi and smile, then turn and walk through his door. Holly's reaction was always the same: heat would rise up her neck, her heart would beat faster, and she'd wish they could get on the same schedule for once.

It felt weird, wrong even, thinking some other guy was cute when Nick had just broken up with her. Memories of him flashed through her mind every now and then—the warmth of his hand on her lower back, the way he would laugh at her jokes, the way his hair felt when she ran her fingers through it. Then a certain pair of green eyes would push their way through. It felt strange that she might be showing interest in him, that she could be smitten with a person she spoke to for only five minutes. Holly had always trusted her gut and right now, she decided to follow these good-natured feelings and see where they took her.

On Friday morning, she tossed on her new daily uniform and went into the kitchen, grabbing her bags for a trip to the grocery store. She passed Kate who sat in her usual spot on the couch, eyes glued to the computer screen, coffee cup in hand.

"Going to the store?" she asked without looking up.

"Yup. I figured this could count as my 'get-out-of-the-house walk' for the day."

"Are you going to walk really slow and take in the scenery? Maybe hoping you'll run into a certain new neighbor?" With this last question, Kate lifted her gaze and gave Holly a smirk.

Holly threw her empty canvas bags at Kate and plopped down on the couch at her side. "Hey, whatever will get me out of my funk, right? You said so yourself, 'Maybe I should start looking again.' "

Kate folded the bag in her lap and handed it back to her. "I just want you to be careful and maybe don't get your hopes up. Just in case he has a girlfriend that we don't know about."

Holly stood. "It feels nice to smile right now and you know, I don't get girlfriend vibes off him. Plus, what are the odds that he's going to the store at the same time as me? My timing must be off with him."

She shrugged and opened the front door to see Luke, his back to her, locking the door of his apartment. He wore a pale green T-shirt and khaki shorts which looked just as good as the jeans she had previously seen him in. He turned and pushed his brown curls out of his eyes which were wide with surprise as he registered her presence in the hallway. "Oh hello. Looks like we're leaving at the same time finally huh?"

Holly looked over her shoulder at Kate, glued to her screen but trying to suppress a smile. She closed the door and looked at Luke. "Yeah, finally on the same schedule. Where are you off to?"

"I'm finally getting some groceries for a decent meal. Can't live off pizza and take out forever. Can I assume you're heading in the same direction?" He gestured to the bags in her hand. "Maybe we can walk together?"

Pleasantly surprised, but not wanting to look too eager, Holly nodded and smiled. The grocery store was just a few blocks away, and the two had no issues filling the entire walk with conversation. She found him quite easy to talk to. He asked questions about the neighborhood, how long had she been here? What did she do for a living?

When she mentioned being in the theater industry, she was surprised to hear that Tommy, a guy she'd worked with on a few occasions and absolutely loved, was his roommate. Luke explained that quarantine had hit his friend hard and that he now spent most of his time on his computer locked in his room, searching for a job. Holly made a mental note to send Tommy a text, to check on him, and possibly get some information about his charming roommate.

Once at the grocery store, as they walked the aisles together, she asked him about his job, where he had moved from, and what he did in his free time.

"Website developer, the West Loop, and I like to play video games and hang out with friends," he said.

She watched him fill his bags with the ingredients

that looked like the makings of a fantastically healthy dinner, whereas her own bag was filled with various cheeses and crackers and a bottle of wine. *Yeah this looks about right,* she thought. At one point, they had both reached for the same box of pasta and their hands brushed. By the time she pulled her hand back, the butterflies in her stomach were in full flight.

On the way back from the store, they walked slowly, Luke asking more about his new neighborhood. "So, do you know anyone outside of the building?"

"Kind of?"

"What do you mean *kind of?* You either know them or you don't," he teased.

"I know the people in the next building over but only because I see them all the time from the porch, I've only met the girls from the first floor. As for the other apartments, it's the kind of relationship where you see them, and they see you, and when you pass them on the street smile and offer a nod of acknowledgement and you don't talk about how you can see into each other's apartments."

This brought a laugh from him, and she felt that warm feeling spread through her chest.

"Do you look into their apartments often?"

"It's hard not to when you're sitting on the porch. Here I'll show you," she explained as they reached the front of their building. "Put away your food, grab your laptop as a prop, and meet me on the back porch in five minutes."

He grinned. "Deal."

Holly raced through her apartment throwing the entire grocery bag into the fridge, quickly reapplied deodorant, fluffed her hair, and grabbed her laptop.

Stopping to take a deep breath, she craned her neck to find Kate in the other room, focused on what looked to be a call for work. She casually went to the back door and opened. Luke was sitting in one of the chairs, laptop open with a glass of water next to him, looking as if he had been working there all morning.

"I've been waiting a while, what took you so long?" he asked innocently.

Failing to suppress her smile, she sat next to him and opened her laptop. "I'm going to ignore that. I see you already have your prop for spying." Pausing, she looked at him. "I hope you know I actually do my work out here; I don't just pretend and look in on people."

He shook his head, pretending to be skeptical. "I don't know, I feel like your real job is detective and answering emails is your 'prop' for that."

Grinning, she pointed across the way. "Okay when you need a moment to collect your thoughts and you want to stare into space you've got three options. When you need a happy moment, look up to the parents-to-be."

They both turned their gaze upward and saw the couple attempting to put together a crib. The wife was smiling and laughing as the husband looked frustrated and kept picking up and dropping various parts.

"When you need to just think about something else entirely, look straight across toward the window on the right. He always is doing something random."

As if on cue, the man across the way walked into his room then closed the door. He moved to the wall and gazed into a mirror, smiling as he grabbed a towel lying on his dresser and wiped something off his cheek. He then took a blue, thin scarf from his pocket and placed it down in front of him.

Luke and Holly shared a look of puzzlement then turned back to the scene. The man started laughing at his expression and turned and walked toward his piano, moving closer to the window. As he moved closer to the window, she squinted. "Is that…is that blood on his cheek?"

She turned to Luke who had the same expression, trying to make it out. "It kind of looks like it. Do you think he cut himself shaving? I mean who just laughs at their reflection with blood on it?"

As they sat there, the previous good-natured vibe disappeared. Both jumped when they heard the man start to play a slow, almost mournful tune on his piano.

Holly cleared her throat. "See, like I said, always random with him. Anyway, onto the window on the left. You can look there when you want to be amused. It's two girls who live there, a bit younger than us, and they're still in the right-out-of-college phase where they do dumb things."

They turned and watched one of the girls pacing back and forth as she spoke on her phone. Looking worried, she hung up, redialed, then repeated the process. Holly turned to him. "Okay, nothing too exciting today but do you see what I mean? Sometimes you can't help but look."

"No, I agree, plus, now all I want to do is wait and see what's happening with the girls. My money is that she's calling the roommate, telling her some drama that has ensued with their friend group." He looked at her and smiled. "I guess we're both just going to have to do our work out here more often to stay up to date."

She settled back into her seat and returned the smile. Maybe 'going to work' for the next few days would, dare she say it, be productive after all. As they settled into a working silence, she glanced back at her neighbors and saw the man on the second floor had stopped playing piano and stared at her and Luke, smiling. A bit unnerved, she gave him a friendly smile and nod, he slowly looked back down and went on playing piano.

Chapter Four

Luke woke the next day with a thrum of excitement running through his body. He had spent most of yesterday with Holly. She was so easy to talk to, to be around. His anxiety about his life—the outside world—it all seemed to melt away when he was around her. They planned to work on the back porch again today, under the guise of keeping tabs on the neighbors. It did not matter to him, he just wanted to be around someone, around her—and to keep having fun.

He got out of bed and shuffled toward the kitchen dressed only in shorts, pausing when he heard the clacking of a keyboard from the living room. Changing direction, he discovered Tommy, furiously typing on his keyboard while the television provided background noise and music blared from the phone sitting on the desk next to him. "Do you want me to bring in another screen or you got enough things on at one time?"

Jumping, his roommate spun in his chair looking sheepish. "Sorry, I guess it's serving as white noise while I redo my cover letter. I hope I didn't wake you."

Waving away his apology, Luke said, "You're fine, man. Let me know if you need help proofreading, editing, or whatever. You seem motivated this morning."

Tommy shrugged his shoulders and gave a lopsided grin. "New place, new motivation? I've got to print this, be right back." He got up and walked out of the room with Luke about to follow as something on the television caused him to stop short. He grabbed the remote and turned the volume up.

"...and in other news, another woman has gone missing in the Lakeview neighborhood. Jennifer Lawler was last seen by her roommate three nights ago."

A picture filled the screen of Jennifer Lawler and her roommate, their arms around each other's shoulders, broad smiles on their faces. It was clearly taken from Facebook, probably snapped when the two had a night out. Realization hit him that he had seen the roommate before, on the phone pacing in her room, just a day ago. *These were the girls who lived across the alley from him.*

He quickly went to the front door, swung it open, rushing across the hall and knocked loudly on Holly's door.

No answer.

He knocked again and heard the shuffling of feet, then suddenly the door swung open with a disheveled Holly on the other side. "Wha— Are you okay?"

"The other roommate, she's missing."

Her expression turned from one of confusion to concern as he grabbed her hand and led her back through his open door.

****

It was one thing to be woken up by loud knocks at the door, but it was another to find a semi-nude Luke, worried and grabbing her arm. His chest was level with her eyeline, and she couldn't help but follow the trail of chest hair down his body. The trail disappeared into a pair of low-hanging black basketball shorts. When he grabbed her hand and pulled her into his apartment, she felt as if she was in a daze.

His apartment was the same layout as hers. Stray boxes filled the room here and there, but she saw a couch, coffee table, and desk all set up. He led her to his television and stopped, pointing at the screen with his right hand while still gripping her hand in his left. Trying to ignore the feel of his strong fingers and the fact that he hadn't let go, Holly tried to focus and was taken aback by a photo of her neighbors with the headline *Missing Girl* on the bottom.

"Oh my God, she's the next one. And it's someone we know...well kind of."

Scared, Holly locked eyes with Luke. After years of reading blogs and listening to podcasts, she knew the horrors that happened in the world but always had that privilege of being personally removed from it. She never knew anyone who had gone to jail, or been involved in a murder, she just read about them. Studying the photo, she wondered how many times she had seen the girls leave their apartment and come back at odd hours, how many times she had walked with them down the street, always together, taking selfies, fixing their hair, their outfits...

Something stuck out in her memory. She turned to him. "Something isn't right."

Luke raised an eyebrow "Well, yeah, Holly. A girl has gone missing."

She let go and placed her hands on her hips "That's not what I mean, I'm talking about the photo. I feel like I'm remembering something but—oh—what is it?" She slowly sank onto the couch, concentrating on that one thought. The picture, the hair, the dresses, the scarf...

"Luke, that scarf...we've seen it recently."

She slowly looked up at him. Yesterday they saw that piece of clothing be placed on a dresser not through the left window where the girls lived, but through the one on the right.

He shook his head, turning off the TV. "No that's crazy. He might have just, I don't know, found it on the ground outside or in their stairwell or…or something."

Holly pressed. "Luke, he was wiping blood off his face. Oh my God. We have to call the police."

He sat down next to her. "Let's not jump to conclusions, okay? Let's take a moment and calm down and—" He looked around his apartment as if trying to find an end to his sentence. In this silence he seemed to finally realize that he was wearing only shorts. "—and put on a shirt. I'm so sorry, I'll be back in a moment." He shot up off the couch and ran into his room. The minute his door closed, another one opened and Tommy came into the room.

"What's happening in here?" His eyes fell on Holly, sitting on his couch. "Holly. This is a surprise. I…You…what are you doing here? And in your pajamas?" he said, laughing.

Glancing down, she realized she'd forgotten she was wearing an oversized T-shirt and pajama shorts. She didn't even want to think about what her curly hair looked like at the moment, probably a rat's nest on top of her head. And she had let Luke see her like this.

Embarrassed, she quickly stood and laughed. "I am so sorry I haven't texted you in a while but, well, hi neighbor." She went over, giving him a big hug. "It's a long story, but I really should get going and put on some real clothes. Luke will explain everything to you."

"Wait how do you know Lu—"

"I'll see you later! Welcome to the building! Bye."

Holly ran out of the apartment and across the hall

back into hers, where she closed and locked the door, leaning against it and letting out a sigh.

This was crazy. One neighbor was missing, and another might be involved. How many times had she looked into that man's bedroom, listened to him play the same sad tune on the same piano, and never suspected a thing? He looked normal, not pale, not gaunt with stringy hair. Nothing how a villain would look like in a movie.

Her fears melted into the back of her mind as different thoughts took center stage, thoughts about Luke and his shirt-lessness.

No, now was not the time to be thinking about her hot neighbor. Now was not the time to think about how he had grabbed her wrist and let his hand slide into her hand and hadn't let go, about how warm and soft his palm felt next to hers. How he sat close to her so that his natural musk engulfed her, and that she could see the individual hairs in his stubble, how they perfectly surrounded his lips. His pink, soft, perfectly kissable lips…

She needed to calm down before her mind wandered so far she wouldn't be able to get work done today. Oh God, work. She was supposed to sit with him on the back porch today and work next to him. She didn't know if she could sit there, knowing that someone across the way was missing, possibly kidnapped or even killed. An idea popped into her head; they did not know if the neighbor man was involved, but what better way to confirm suspicions before calling the police than by having a stakeout? The man had seen them sitting out there yesterday so he wouldn't think anything of it if they proceeded to sit out there today and he would go about living his normal life. The porch provided the perfect cover.

She sprang into action, quickly changing from her pajamas into jeans and a T-shirt, finger combed her curls into being somewhat presentable, and put on a bit of mascara. She rushed back through her apartment throwing the door open heading back across the hall this time knocking on the door rather than being dragged through it.

Tommy opened the door with a smile. "Long time no see, but what's going on?"

Before she could answer she heard Luke yell from the next room. "I'm going to go see if she's all right, I probably scared her off." He walked into view while pulling a shirt over his head. He abruptly stopped in his tracks with a look of surprise on his face at seeing Holly standing in the doorway.

"You didn't scare me off, but I just thought of something. We have to stay outside and see if Second Window does something suspicious."

Still standing between the two, Tommy asked, "Second Window?"

"The guy who lives across the alley, the second window in from the left. She thinks he's a murderer," Luke responded. "—I think he's just weird."

She frowned. "But we won't know for sure unless we keep an eye on him. That scarf could be a trophy from his victim. It fits."

"Holly—"

She cut him off. "Just indulge me. Meet me out there in a few."

Turning, she marched back into her apartment to gather her things. She felt determined to follow her gut.

****

Hours passed and nothing strange presented itself. Every time Holly saw movement through the second-floor window, she would tense up, bracing herself for the sight of a dead body, a murder weapon, or something generally nefarious.

Instead, it seemed to be a normal day for Second Window, sitting on the computer or playing the piano. What proved to be more difficult than spying on a supposed murderer was watching the roommate of the missing girl on the first floor go about her day. The police came by and appeared to ask more questions which made her cry on and off.

Holly couldn't help but imagine how she would react if their roles were reversed; if it had been her, and Kate was missing, how helpless and sad she would feel. As the day passed, she grew worried that Luke would start to think she was a bit crazy for making him watch the neighbors. He sat and worked with her but had been quieter than before. Every time she looked over, his eyes would flicker from the window to her then down to his screen. Maybe she had listened to too many stories. Maybe she wanted so badly to find someone to blame for such a terrible crime that she was looking at anyone.

She closed her computer and twisted in her seat so she could face Luke. "Listen, if you want to go inside and work, you can. I think I was so worked up this morning and jumped to conclusions."

He mirrored her actions, matching her gaze. "I think we were both worked up this morning, but I don't really want to go inside. I've been thinking, the news aired this morning, and that story has run on every news cycle, police have been into the building." He leaned closer, lowering his voice. "And he hasn't done anything out of the ordinary."

Holly leaned in. "I know. He's boring to watch."

He closed his eyes and shook his head. "That's just it, he should've reacted to something. Cops are in your building, yet you don't look out the window to see what's going on? You possibly collect a blue scarf in your building and see that it belonged to a missing girl and you don't try to give it back to her roommate or tell her something?" He leaned back and crossed his arms over his impressive chest. "He's acting *too* boring."

She sat, stunned; he was right. Second Window had not displayed any reaction to anything all day. His windows were cracked, and blinds were open, he could not be oblivious to the activity happening below and yet he ignored it. A slow smile spread on her face; she had been right.

Luke leaned back in. "I had another thought as well. We've been watching him during business hours, we've got to assume he has a job and is actually doing it so he wouldn't have time during the day to do any bad guy stuff. What we need to do is monitor him after hours. What do you say we meet back out here tonight and continue our stakeout?"

Holly pondered his suggestion. "Okay, but what is our cover? When he looks over, he's just going to see the two of us sitting here staring at him?"

He smiled with mischief in his eyes. "Would you like to come over for dinner at my place tonight? I've got a back porch we could turn into an open-air dining opportunity."

Chapter Five

Holly sat at her desk, staring into her lighted makeup mirror. She had a date with Luke tonight. Could she really call it a date when it was under the guise of a stakeout? They'd decided to meet back on the porch at seven, pretending to be on a date when they'd be spying on a possible murderer. They were putting on a show for Second Window, should he look their way. For that, she had to dress the part.

She could not remember the last time she had been on a date that had not meant sitting on her couch, ordering in, and watching a movie. Yes, this would be taking place just ten feet away, but this felt completely different. She had someone who was cooking for her, she had someone to dress up for and who wanted to dress up and look their best for her. It was bringing her life.

Feeling like a teenager, she had tried on three separate outfits before getting Kate's input. She finally decided on a black cotton wrap-around dress that stopped just above her knees. The short, loose sleeves came into a tightened, low-cut bodice which flared out around her hips. It was a good summer date dress, and it was the first time she had the opportunity to wear it in a long time. She wore her hair down with a section pinned back, this hair and the black dress made her feel like she was the femme fatal in a noir movie, a look she felt was appropriate for the occasion. Her recently tanned skin mixed with the summer heat led her to keep her makeup light, opting for concealer instead of foundation with just a bit of mascara and black eyeliner. She completed her look with a pair of small drop-down crystal earrings and a few bangle charm bracelets and now here she sat, staring at her reflection, unable to wrap her head around the whirlwind that had been the past few days.

A part of her felt slightly disappointed. She had to remind herself this night was a cover, a deception. This desire for the date to be real, for a genuine connection with Luke, surprised her. She never bounced back this quickly after a breakup and somehow this, whatever this was with him, had snuck up on her. Usually when she felt ready to date again, she would go about it slowly, she would download a few apps, make the profiles and start chatting when she felt up to it. This kind of thing didn't happen to her, her life wasn't a romantic comedy.

A knock on her bedroom door snapped her out of the mental downward spiral and back to the present. A grinning Kate poked her head through the opening. "Judging by what I just saw outside, I cannot wait for you to tell me all about this date. Of course I'll need all the details on how good the kissing is."

With butterflies in her stomach, Holly hurried past Kate to the back door that led to the porch and gasped. String lights covered the small area making it a bright spot in a sea of darkness. A small thin blanket had draped over the patio table and a daisy stood in water right in the middle along with two bottle of red wine, ready to be poured all out, for her.

Taking in the scene in from hear her friend come up behind her whispered, "Go. Have fun." Giving her a gentle push over the threshold, she closed the door behind her. Holly, in all her gracefulness, stumbled. Righting herself, she turned and stuck out her tongue at a smirking Kate.

"Oh, you're here."

Holly quickly put her tongue back in her mouth and spun around.

Luke stood in his doorway holding a plate, looking almost ethereal surrounded by the string lights. He wore a white shirt with several buttons undone, allowing her a peek of chest hair. The sleeves were rolled up to his elbows exposing his muscular forearms, and on the bottom he wore a pair of dark jeans. He trimmed his facial hair and had managed to tame his unruly curls. The lights around him made his green eyes sparkle.

"I was going to come knock on your door and escort you…well out to here."

She gaped at the plate of bruschetta in his hand. "This is all incredible, how did you have time to do this? We separated only a few hours ago."

"The good thing is that when you move, all your holiday decoration boxes are already out so I took advantage of that and gave us some mood lighting. Plus, I thought maybe it would help us see better." He tilted his head in the direction of the neighboring building. She looked over into Second Window's window, he was sitting on the end of his bed, his attention on the television in front of him.

Luke's voice brought her back. "Looks like he'll be ￼ for a while."

Claiming her usual chair, Holly sat. "So, we've got to waste."

"ꞌ hope you don't think of it as a waste, we've got a

purpose here." He placed the food down and sat opposite her. "Plus, I cooked us a proper meal and it's been so long since I've had that pleasure, so you sit and enjoy yourself at least for a little bit."

She laughed as she reached for an appetizer. "Oh I'm definitely excited about that part. Can I ask what you've made for us?" She bit into the small crostini and her eyes went wide. "If it's as good as this, I can tell you I'm already excited."

Leaning over, he opened the bottle of wine, pouring them each a portion. "Since it's been a long time, I decided to really go for it. I got us steaks and shrimp with creamed spinach and mashed potatoes on the side. It might be too much…"

Holly snorted into her wine glass. "You've never seen me eat."

He chuckled, looking back through the screen door into his kitchen. "I've got a few minutes before I have to rotate all the food. Tell me something about yourself, how did you come to live here?"

She stared into the wineglass for several moments. "I've lived in a few apartments all over the city. I've been in Chicago since college and just love it, I've never wanted to leave. Every few years, it's nice to get a change of neighborhoods and upgrade a bit. Thankfully, Kate has always needed a roommate too. I met her in college, and we've been best friends ever since. I'm sure it will all change within the next two years though, she's had a long-term boyfriend who has been living in Boston for the past year, for his job, and it's looking like he might move back. So they'll be looking for a new place together when that happens."

Holly was avoiding these thoughts a lot. If she didn't

think about it, it wasn't going to happen. Of course, she was so happy for Kate and Ben, she was excited that they would finally get to live together but it meant being on her own for the first time. Truly alone, and that thought frightened her. "How about you?"

"I have actually been living on my own for a long time. I used to really like it, having my own space. I liked the freedom to come and go when I wanted; to stay in and be alone for as long as I needed then go out when I needed social interaction. Recently however…it has been hard on me. Not having that option to go out anymore really made me anxious, it was getting worse and worse until Tommy told me he needed to move. You know, with venues closed he couldn't afford to live by himself anymore, so I jumped at the chance. It is kind of perfect, I'm saving a bit of money, I get to live with my best friend and help him." He waved his hand at the building next to them. "I get to meet new people…"

When a kitchen timer rang out from inside the kitchen, Luke stood. "Give me a minute to make sure everything is looking good. Please, keep eating."

After he ran into the apartment, she watched through the door as he put on oven mitts and bent over, checking the food in the oven, giving her an excellent view of his butt in those jeans.

God, this man was beautiful. He was open, honest, a good cook, it all felt too good to be true. He turned around, causing her to quickly snap her eyes back up to his. "It's looking good. Just a few more minutes." He came back out and sat down.

Holly asked, "What's Tommy doing for dinner?"

"Probably ordering pizza and hopefully staying on the other side of the apartment. Do you normally ask about other men on fake dates?"

Holly, who had just shoved another crostini into her mouth, tried to backtrack but he just shook his head, smiling. "I'm just kidding. So, I never asked for more details about these missing girls?"

She filled him in on the missing girls' names, ages, and the fact that they all lived relatively close to one another. In the middle of this briefing, she paused so Luke could bring the food out. In between bites of one of the most delicious meals she had ever had, she continued the story then started talking about the *MfYT* blog in general.

She told him how R.J. wrote in a style that made her feel like a friend, as if she was telling her a story over drinks. How she loved hearing the stories where the bad guys get caught or get what's coming to them. She rounded back to the missing ladies' case. "I'm sorry I've been talking so much, but it's crazy to me that this is happening in our own backyard. I've always taken comfort in the fact that I don't know anyone in the stories I read or hear, that I can almost pretend they're not real, and now it's just—it's unnerving."

He reached out and covered her left hand with his right and gave it a squeeze. Surprised at the butterflies the action gave her, she glanced up and saw the serious look on his face and flushed. "I've got your back. You won't be getting taken anytime soon, and speaking of being taken..." He looked over at the next building. "We haven't been monitoring him all that closely."

Holly tore her eyes away from his and saw Second Window Man moving about his bedroom, apparently cleaning and rearranging things.

"You keep watching," he said. "I'll grab dessert."

"You made dessert, too?"

"I'm putting ice cream into bowls so I'm making it easier for us to eat." He grinned, and her heart fluttered. "Eyes back on the target, please?"

Holly continued to watch Second Window Man clean. For the first time she really took stock of his appearance. He was tall and lanky, probably over six feet tall. He wore his thin sandy blond hair a bit shaggy. His flannel shirt seemed too big for him, as if he had lost weight. She watched as he lifted a heavy box onto his bed, opened the cardboard flaps, and smiled down at the contents.

The door opened and Luke stepped out, carrying two bowls. "Totally and completely handmade—not really—ice cream." He placed her bowl on the table in front of her and returned to his seat.

Lowering her voice, she said, "Second Window Man seems to have found whatever he was looking for."

Turning in unison, they watched their neighbor slowly take things out of the box. The first was a red, wool hat, followed by a wallet, then a case for eyeglasses and finally a pair of sunglasses. He placed each item carefully on his bed, then turned and picked up the blue scarf and brought it to his nose. After visibly inhaling, he closed his eyes as if savoring the aroma.

Straightening in her chair, Holly grabbed Luke's hand. "I think that's a box of his trophies. Things he takes from each girl he…" She trailed off, not wanting to finish the sentence.

Second Window Man placed the scarf in the box and slowly, one-by-one, replaced the items back in the box. She felt her breath quicken. "Oh my God this is it, this is proof." Her voice rose from a whisper to a near shout.

"We need to do something. We need to call the police."

Still holding her hand, Luke spoke in a low, warning tone. "Holly, calm down. We don't want to let him know we were watching hi—"

Not taking her eyes off the window across the alley, Holly's voice pitched even higher, "I have to get my phone. I—" She stopped as two things happened at once:

Second Window Man stopped placing things in his box and turned toward a commotion occurring outside the building. Holly waited to make eye contact with him, the man she was clearly watching, the man who she was now one hundred percent sure was a killer.

In that moment, Luke leaned over the table, taking his hand out of her grip, and placing it on her cheek. He turned her head toward his and kissed her.

It took her a moment to react. She closed her eyes and slowly brought her hand up to his face to cup his cheek, her fingers brushing over his stubble and settling into his hair. Without meaning to, she opened her lips slightly and Luke immediately deepened the kiss, taking her mouth as he stood and moved around the table, bringing Holly with him. She followed, not knowing how her legs managed to work, letting him pull her toward him.

Her mind went blank, and she felt like she was floating. Then all at once, her mind exploded with a thousand thoughts.

Luke is kissing me. Oh my God he is kissing me. He is such a good kisser. His lips feel amazing. What is that cologne he is wearing? He tastes like vanilla ice cream. Oh God what is he thinking?

And then as soon as it started, it ended. He gently pulled away causing her eyelids to flutter open. He hovered just a few inches away from her, still cupping her face. She felt disappointed to see his beautiful green eyes not looking at her but instead, toward the window.

"Okay, it looks like Second Window Man has lost interest in watching a couple kiss. He's putting the box back in his closet." His eyes flicked back to her, he cleared his throat. "I'm sorry, it's just that he was about to look at us and we were not being subtle. I figured that would be a good way to not look like we were spying."

Holly, still searching for her voice, nodded dumbly as he slowly released her from his hold. She backed away, smoothing out her dress, and took a shaky breath. Finally trusting her voice not to waver, she said, "No I think that was a great save. I'm sorry I almost blew our whole operation, the kiss definitely worked."

She could not look him in the eye, she didn't want him to sense her disappointment that the kiss was over and was only intended to shut her up. Wanting to busy herself, she began gathering the dishes and said, "Let me help clean up."

"No, you really don't have to—"

"Please," she argued. "You cook; I clean—or at least load your dishwasher." She smiled, and once more, they were back to the lighthearted banter. "Plus, I think we should go inside and maybe plan what we should do next?" Without waiting for a response, she nodded her head, her arms ladened with dishes, toward the door. He quickly opened it; she marched into his kitchen.

Chapter Six

Needing a moment in order to clear his head, Luke let her walk into the kitchen while he lingered, gathering the rest of the glasses and dishes left on the table.

That kiss had been, well, amazing. It had been a long time since he was intimate with someone, but he never remembered anything feeling like that. It had happened in a moment of panic, watching her spiral into hysteria, looking at the man across the way; instinct took over and he leaned in. He angled them at first so that he could look and see if Second Window was watching. He was glad Holly's eyes were closed because Second Window watched them for a creepy amount of time, smiling.

It was why Luke deepened the kiss. But as soon as they stood up and she moved closer to him, his senses melted away. He forgot the man watching across the way and let himself savor the moment. He had enjoyed the feeling of her soft, full lips on his, the way her fingers wound themselves into the hair at the nape of his neck, the way she clung to him as if he was the anchor she needed to stay put. He had wanted it to go on forever. He had wanted to continue the date, to bring her straight to his bedroom and for neither one of them to come up for air for a long time...

That is when his brain jump started. His eyes had flown open and immediately looked across the way to see the man had gone back to moving things around.

That was when it hit him, what he had impulsively done, and started to back away to bring them both back into the present.

As he walked through the door, he found Holly rinsing and putting items into the dishwasher. It didn't feel strange, seeing her in his kitchen. While most things had been put away from the move, the room still felt new, but seeing her there somehow made him feel more at home. Walking up next to her, he placed the glasses down on the counter. She seemed to be focusing hard on her task, avoiding his gaze and increasing his doubt about the kiss.

Did I made a huge mistake?

"I'm sorry if that was not okay. I didn't even think— I should have asked."

Confusion flashed across her face as she looked up at him. "You don't have to be sorry. It's totally okay. I mean thank you for apologizing but I'm not offended, or anything. I'm—" She cut herself off mid-sentence, looking flustered. She bent her head down and grabbed the glasses to rinse them off.

She's what? What was she and why did she stop herself? He so desperately wanted her to finish her sentence, to say that maybe the spark that he felt had not been one-sided. He moved away, giving her space, and grabbed two beers from the fridge. He opened one placing it next to her and leaned against the wall directly behind her. She looked over her shoulder and asked, "So you saw what he did right? He very creepily sniffed that scarf and put it in that box. That is not normal."

"I agree—" Luke began, but Holly kept going, turning her attention back to her task as she continued speaking.

"It's what serial killers do; they keep items from each victim. They save them so they can remember and revisit the memory. In some cases, they actually do revisit the bodies or something; they can't help it." Without stopping for a breath, she asked, "Do you think we can tell the police to just go and look for the box?"

It took Luke a moment to realize she had asked him a question, or that she'd turned around to face him. He had been transfixed by her curls that bounced with every movement she made.

He quickly took a sip of beer to recover before he responded. "I think we can call in a tip but that's about it. There is no tangible evidence for the police to probably even enter his house or something like that."

Holly's brow furrowed in thought as she grabbed for her beer and tilted her head back to take a big swig. Luke's eyes followed the movement down to the neckline of her dress and then immediately shook his head. What was wrong with him? They were talking about a possible kidnapper and killer who lived just across the alley and all he could think about was what Holly was wearing underneath her dress. He pushed off the wall and grabbed his phone from his pocket.

"Let's do this together."

He dialed the non-emergency number, putting it on speaker so they could both hear and sat at his kitchen table. Holly followed suit sitting on the edge of her seat, across the table from him. Without thinking, Luke reached out and put his hand over hers. She offered a grateful smile, and he felt a zing go right through him of something he could not quite name.

They explained to the operator what they had seen and what they believed it meant. The operator promised the police would be notified and would send someone to check out the tip.

After hanging up, they sat in silence, processing everything that had happened that night. The moment ended when they heard a banging from the other side of the apartment and Holly jumped. He squeezed her hand in a sign of comfort and he rolled his eyes. "Tommy must be having a party in his room or something."

As if summoned, his roommate appeared in the kitchen wearing green sweatpants and a gray T-shirt. Tommy stopped dead in his tracks like a deer in headlights when he realized the two of them were sitting in front of him. "I'm sorry, I didn't realize recon was still happening."

Looking at Holly, Luke said, "I had to tell him about the plan." He turned to his roommate, and said, "It actually just ended. We saw a suspicious deed and reported it."

His friend looked relieved. "Oh good. I didn't want to interrupt."

Aware of Tommy's focus on their hands, Luke quickly pulled back and stood abruptly. Turning to Holly, he said, "Do you want to stay and hang out? We can all watch a movie and have another drink."

She stood up, finishing her beer. "I should probably get back to my place. You know, to fill Kate in on all the details and such. I had a great time tonight, pretending to be on a date." She snaked her arms around his waist and gave him a quick hug which he briefly returned, catching a whiff of her citrus scent, before she pulled away.

"I had a great pretend date, too. Want to work on the porch tomorrow and watch justice be served with me?"

She looked up and smiled. "I'd love that." With a

wave to Tommy, she went out the back door and a moment later the screen door slammed shut, breaking the silence.

Luke turned to see Tommy standing there with a sly expression on his face and arms crossed. "That did not seem like a pretend date to me. She dressed up for you. Did you see her dress?"

Of course he had seen the dress, he had been actively reminding himself to keep his eyes on her face almost the whole night. Luke waved off the comment and went about starting the dishwasher. "Neither she nor I made any mention of there being a second date. Or I mean a first real date? Whatever, you know what I mean."

Flustered, he grabbed his beer and headed toward the living room; Tommy followed. "You were holding hands. You cooked for her. You never cook for me."

Luke flopped onto the couch, grabbing the remote and putting on an old baseball game. "That's because you don't go about trying to catch murderers with me." Under his breath said, "Or look that good in a dress."

Tommy shook his head and sat down next to him. Turning his attention to the game, Luke tried not to think about the kiss.

****

Holly went into her apartment and straight to the couch, startling Kate who was kneeling on her yoga mat with her arms outstretched. Turning only her head, she acknowledged Holly with an expectant look on her face.

Holly put her hands over her face and let out a frustrated sound. "It was so good. He was so…good."

Eyes wide, Kate bolted up from the floor onto the couch. "I am going to need more details please, Ben has been gone so long, I need to live vicariously through you.

I can't even remember what real dates are like anymore."

Holly threw her hands in the air. "That's the thing, it wasn't a date. It was a pretend date." She filled Kate in on everything she had seen across the alley, talking fast, letting the story spill out. Her friend listened closely when she described each item taken out of the box and celebrated when Holly told her about the kiss.

"Oh my God, how was it?"

Holly stood making her way to her room. "It doesn't matter how good it was. It was strictly to get me to shut up and for us to not get caught. I don't think it meant anything to him."

"But what about what it meant to you?"

"What matters is that we're hopefully going to help put a total creep behind bars. Anyways, let me go get changed and I'll come join you."

She went into her room and changed into her pajamas, her thoughts focused on the not date that had just occurred.

That kiss definitely meant something to her, but the question was, did he feel it too? The way he had held her, shielding her from prying eyes, made her feel safe. Switching her train of thought, she moved to her window, opening the blinds, and looked out onto the street. Would the police come and perform their promised check? She'd have to keep her eyes and ears open for any sign of them.

Letting the blinds fall back down she turned to go back out into the living room determined to enjoy the rest of her night, or at least try to.

Chapter Seven

Holly woke with a mixture of emotions stemming from the previous night. Though she was excited to see Luke again, she still felt flustered from that kiss. She was scared that Second Window Man may find out that they had called the cops on him and overall, she was anxious to see what happened today. She lay in bed, trying to sift through her thoughts for a while until finally getting up and getting ready for the day.

July was fast approaching the Windy City, and it was getting too hot for leggings or jeans, so she opted for a flowy, navy-blue sundress for the day. Her hair still had the product in it from the night before so she just finger-combed the tangles out.

Yelling a quick good morning to Kate and grabbing a cup of coffee, she went outside to the porch only to be greeted with a surprise.

There Luke sat, cup in hand and computer on his lap. The string lights still hung from the ceiling, clinking lightly together as a warm breeze blew through. Resting on the table was a carafe of coffee, a sleeve of bagels with a tub of cream cheese and two plates. Luke stood and went in for a hug. Holly, hands still full, tried to hug back and inwardly kicked herself for being so awkward. She felt enveloped by the smell of his body wash and cologne as his tall frame embraced her. She found the mixture of fresh scent and spicy teakwood intoxicating.

"Good morning. Just in case, I figured we should keep up appearances. Plus, I was really craving bagels. I hope you like them."

If she was unsure of how she felt for Luke before, it was confirmed now. Bagels were a sure-fire way to her heart, and she desperately hoped she could play it cool. "Oh my God yes." He jumped a little at the enthusiasm and laughed. They both sat down and started on breakfast.

"So, do you think we'll see a raid today?"

Without missing a beat, he replied, "Tactical teams? Battering rams on doors? A standoff?"

"I'm serious."

Luke put down his bagel. "I think we need to wait and see. Maybe, monitor the situation, and if we don't see anything we call again?"

Satisfied with this answer, she turned her attention back to her meal. Once finished, they settled into a comfortable silence, both doing work on their own. Only the sounds of the clinking of computer keys and the twinkling lights above lightly hitting each other filled the space.

After a few hours, and Holly was rereading an email for the second time—the first time she'd been too distracted by Luke's arms as he moved his portable mouse all over the table—excitement entered the picture. A police car pulled up in front of the neighboring building. Looking to her left, she saw that Luke had also noticed the police presence.

"Keep working," he said. "Let's not make it look like we're too interested."

Nodding, she bent her head as if to look at her screen all the while keeping her eyes on the street. Moments later, they heard a faint knocking through the open window and saw Second Window Man rush out of his room, presumably to answer the door.

Holly sat very still, barely breathing. They weren't so close as to hear what was being said but she could tell they were all talking. After a while, Second Window Man led the cops into his bedroom. His body language was open and inviting. Holly guessed he was letting them look around freely.

The cops poked around a bit while he kept chatting. One made their way to the closet and as they opened the door, she held her breath, unable to tear her eyes away.

She heard Luke say under his breath, "It's okay." She exhaled looking at him, his eyes also glued to the window across the way. She felt comforted knowing he was just as concerned.

The cop, doing a once over, gestured to a box on the floor of the closet. Second Window moved past and picked it up, placing it on the bed.

"Here we go," Luke said, again in almost a whisper.

The police officer opened the cardboard flaps of the box and looked in, he grabbed something and lifted it up to inspect…a book. Holly watched, confused, as the policeman picked up one book after another. It was the wrong box, it had to be. She looked over at Luke who sat with a furrowed brow, staring intently at the window. The policeman put everything back into the box and placed it back in the closet. Both officers proceeded to look around once more then left the bedroom and out of their line of sight. After ten minutes, the pair witnessed the cops leaving out the front of the building.

As they walked to their squad car, Holly turned to Luke. "Why didn't they find it? What has he done with the box and the things in it?"

He sat staring into space, as if lost in thought. "I have no idea."

Holly looked back across the alley into the room. Second Window had moved to the piano and starting to play the slow tune, smiling to himself. As if feeling her stare, he looked up, making eye contact with her. Unsure what to do, she smiled back, giving him a nod. He acknowledged her back and held eye contact until she felt forced to break it. Turning to Luke, she reached out her hand and without questioning, he took it bringing it to his lips, brushing it with a gentle kiss before resting their intwined hands on the table.

All the while the Second Window Man kept looking at her. Smiling.

A few minutes passed when Holly made an excuse about wanting some lunch and went inside. She kept her head down that whole time but as she walked into the apartment she happened to look up and saw Second Window staring out the window, right at her. Ducking her head, she waited to relax until the walls of her apartment shielded her from the creepy, prying eyes. Grabbing a clementine from the fridge, she walked into the other room and plopped down on the couch next to her roommate.

"He's hidden them."

Kate, not looking away from her screen, said, "What? Is Luke 'hiding' his feelings about you?"

Holly shifted position, bringing her feet beneath her. "No, Second Floor. He's hiding his trophies. The police were just there, and they left. It looks like they didn't find anything and…and I think he knows we were the ones who called. He…he was staring at me and smiling."

This made Kate tear her eyes away from her screen and look at her inquisitively. She turned her body on the couch to fully face her. "He was staring at you?" Holly nodded which caused Kate to look even more distressed. "I really don't like that, Hol. Maybe I should postpone my trip this weekend. I'm not crazy about leaving you alone."

She forgot her roommate's plan to see her boyfriend, Ben, this coming weekend. They were both renting cars and planned to meet in a place that was equidistant to Chicago and Boston which happened to be Silver Creek, New York. When Holly asked what exactly they were going to do in Silver Creek, New York, Kate had simply laughed. She had taken that to mean the couple would not be leaving their room all weekend long.

Holly stood, waving away Kate's concern. "There is absolutely no way I am letting you postpone this trip. You haven't seen Ben in ages, and you have been working way too hard to not take the time off. Plus, you know what? I'm sick of you and seeing your face all the time. I definitely need the apartment to myself." She said this last bit with her lips turned up at the corner, letting her roommate know she was teasing.

She smiled sympathetically. "I appreciate that, but it doesn't mean that I'm not worried about you. Can you maybe go see your parents or something while I'm away?"

"Don't worry, I'll make plans, keep myself busy."

Kate got up and gave Holly a hug, whispering in a teasing tone, "Maybe you should make plans with Luke."

She pushed her back and gave her a playful hit on the arm. Going into her room, she closed the door still thinking about it. Maybe she should ask Luke to hang out this weekend, she had to show him that she too could cook...

****

Luke barely got any work done because he couldn't stop thinking about how Second Window Man had watched Holly. She had kept her head down which seemed to make the man more determined to make eye contact with her. It was not until she went inside that he finally moved away from the window and went on with his day. It made Luke uneasy that right after the police had left, Second Window had turned his attention toward them, almost as if he knew that it was them that had caused the police visit.

He looked down at his watch. Holly had been inside for quite a while, and with each passing minute his disappointment grew as the chances of her rejoining him lessened. It had only been two weeks since they first met although it felt like so much longer. He liked her company, her wit, her easy smile, and that kiss... He wanted to protect her, to help her, to be with her.

The realization startled him. He'd never wanted to be with someone so fast. Throughout his dating history his relationships usually started as a slow burn, taking his time to warm up to someone before wanting to commit. Maybe it was the months of isolation or just the excitement of finding a murderer that made him feel these unfamiliar things but, maybe not. Being with Holly felt different.

With that final thought lingering, he got up and knocked on her back door. He was determined to make sure she wasn't afraid to sit outside and, on a more selfish note, he certainly wasn't going to let Second Window spoil the only time he had with her.

A moment later, a willowy blonde opened the door, a knowing smile on her face. "Holly is in her room. Come on in."

He walked past her into the kitchen. Though their apartments had the same floorplans, the similarities ended there. He felt a warmth and a sense of the small space being well-loved. Pots and pans hung from a wire rack attached to the wall with decorative vines woven in between. Well used cookbooks sat stacked in the corner of the counter with a basket of fresh fruits next to them.

Moving into the main room, Luke smiled. Like the kitchen, it felt lived-in and cozy. He saw Holly's influences in the décor, the warm tones of the couch and rug, the wall art that while seemingly random, somehow worked together.

He turned back to the blonde. "We've never actually met, but Holly talks about you a lot. I'm Luke."

Walking past him toward the couch, she snorted out a laugh. "Ha, I know who you are, but yes, hi, I am Kate." She called out in a fake southern accent, "Holly, you have a gentleman caller out here."

Luke immediately felt his face get hot. "Oh no, no I'm not—" His protests were cut short by the door to his right opening and Holly walking out cautiously. He instantly smiled and the warmth left his face, settling into his chest, his heart beating erratically.

"I'm sorry for coming over, I just…you said you were going in for lunch and it's been a while so… I just wanted to make sure that you were okay because I know we weren't expecting that to happen today with Second Window and I didn't like how he was staring at you—erm I mean us and just…"

He trailed off and looked down at his feet. "And I

guess I didn't need to tell you all that."

Holly stood there, a grin slowly spreading across her face. She stared up into his eyes for a moment and then asked, "Would you like to come over for dinner tomorrow?"

Before he could answer, Kate chimed in from the couch. "I'm leaving her all alone this weekend so it would make me feel a lot better if someone was here to make sure this Second Window Man doesn't creep her out or worse."

Luke laughed and turned to Holly. "I would love to come over tomorrow."

Her phone rang. She looked at it and rolled her eyes. "Sorry, this is a call for work. I have to take it. Come over tomorrow at six." She ran back into her room, answering her phone and leaving him standing in the middle of the room, smiling.

She just asked him out. On a date. Alone. No stakeout required.

Chapter Eight

Before Kate left the next morning, she gave Holly a big hug. "I know you will, but just…please be careful."

Holly assured her that she would and sent her off with a wave. Now alone in the apartment, she went to her room and lay down on her bed, having not slept well the night before. At first, she chalked it up to excitement for her date with Luke. It was going to be real and fun and—since she had the place to herself—maybe it would last until the next morning.

Excitement then turned to anxiety when Second Window Man's smile creeped its way into her thoughts, erasing all traces of Luke's perfect green eyes. All night long her mind had stayed on a cycle of wondering what the man across the alley knew, why he looked at her the way he did, and if she was now on the list of his potential victims.

After she landed on that last thought, she immediately scolded herself for being ridiculous. Then, trying to clear her thoughts, she started over again at the beginning. It proved to be an exhausting night.

With no possibility of getting any more sleep, she got up, slipped into workout gear, and started a deep clean on the apartment, one of many things she had put on the mental to-do list before Luke arrived for dinner tonight. She swept and mopped, went about vacuuming every rug, and made sure the entire apartment smelled lovely, aided by multiple candles.

By the time she was happy with how her apartment looked, half the day was gone, and she found herself still needing to go to the grocery store. She decided to make a spicy chicken and pasta dish for dinner. While not the healthiest of meals, she was sure it would impress Luke. After a quick shower, she grabbed her bags and made her way out of the building onto the sidewalk.

Once outside she paused, wanting to make sure she had her wallet and grocery list, when someone called out, "Oh, hello neighbor."

Turning at the sound, she saw Second Window walking over to her from the direction of his building. She had never been this close to him, having only seen him across the alley. Up close, he looked older; she'd put him at late thirties, maybe early forties. He wore a gray T-shirt beneath a thin red flannel, dark jeans, and sneakers. A slight wind blew his thin blond hair off his face as he came up to her.

Trying to hide her initial panic, Holly spoke in the calmest voice she could manage. "Oh, hi. You live in the building next to me, right?"

His smile made her uneasy. His thin lips turned up at the corners, yet his eyes remained without emotion. "Yes, I've seen you outside my window on your porch. My name is Phil. I figured I should introduce myself, so we don't keep making awkward eye contact."

He acted the part of the charming neighbor. Holly didn't fall for it for one second. Though she did not want to be anywhere near this man any longer than necessary, her Midwestern roots kicked in, telling her to be polite.

"Ah yes, I like working out there when the weather is nice. I'm Holly. It's nice to meet you, but I'm just on my way out now."

Putting his hands in his pockets in what she assumed was an attempt to look disarming, he asked, "Oh I was just heading out, too. Do you mind if I walk with you?"

She froze. If she said no, what would stop him from following her? It was only one block, it was broad daylight and she had taken kickboxing a few times, she could do this.

"I'm only going to the store so not too far to walk but um, yeah sure."

She turned and started at a quick pace; his long legs fell into step beside her easily. "So do you live there alone?" he asked. "I never see a roommate out there on your porch, just you."

"Oh um yes, I have a roommate." She paused, trying desperately to think of something the exact opposite of what he wanted to hear. "Her boyfriend is always over— and so is mine—so it just feels like a constant stream of people in and out. You know, always busy."

Holly wondered if he could tell she was lying. Glancing over at him, his eyes were glued to the sidewalk, but he maintained the thin smile on his face. Did he find her amusing?

"Yes, that does sound busy. I don't know if you can tell, but it's just me in my apartment and it can get a bit lonely. I try to get out a lot, meet new people. It's been very hard during the pandemic, but I've found ways to make friends. I guess it's another reason I wanted to introduce myself, just trying to put myself out there."

The fine hair on the back of her neck started to stand up, particularly after he asked, "How long have you and your boyfriend been dating? I happened to see you on a date the other night. Did he just move in? You know, it's hard not to notice moving trucks when you live on a quiet street."

He chuckled again, the sound putting her on edge. She wished he would stop. "Oh just...a while." She was trying to keep her responses short and sweet; she did not want him to know anything about her life.

"That's nice to hear. It's good to have someone around during these times. It can get rather lonely, and I feel that this prolonged solitude has made people extremely dangerous. You never know what is going on. More robberies on our street, more women being attacked..." He let his words hang in the air and, despite the hot July air, chilled Holly to the bone.

The walk to the store was almost over; she was close to ending this conversation. She came to a halt and turned toward him, terrified. He tilted his head, looking at her through the top of his eyes. "Just in case something were to happen. It's good to know who's watching your back. Well I see we've arrived at your destination. Thank you for letting me walk with you. I'm sure we'll see more and more of each other now that we've been properly introduced."

"Yes, I'll see you around."

She turned quickly and walked through the doors behind her. She dared to look over her shoulder and saw Phil standing there, hands clasped together, smiling and watching as the automatic doors closed.

All throughout her time in the store, Holly kept looking over her shoulder, expecting to see Phil standing there, wearing that unsettling smile. Quickly grabbing and paying for her supplies, paranoia followed on the walk home.

He knows that I know. He knows that I've been

watching him, and he basically revealed that he's been watching me, too.

She would not be surprised if he had seen Kate leave this morning. As she reached her apartment building, mind working on all gears, not really looking where she was going, she walked right into Tommy who was walking out at the same time.

"Whoa. Are you all right?" He steadied her as she teetered backward upon impact, her groceries clattering to the ground. "Mind somewhere else today?"

She put her hands over her eyes and took a steadying breath for a moment as he bent down and started picking up her fallen groceries.

"I'm so sorry, Tommy." She bent down and helped him gather up the remaining items. "Are you okay?"

They stood, and he looked into her eyes, concerned. "Are you okay?" he asked again. "You look frazzled."

Holly shook her head. "I just am a little on edge today. I really need to relax before tonight."

He grinned. "You excited for your big date? I heard you asked him this time."

Her body loosened up as she gave him a small, shy smile. "I did. I don't want to be one of those girls but...has he said anything about tonight?"

He handed her the final bag and began to move past her. "I can't betray my best friend's feelings, even to you." He turned back around after walking a few paces. "But I can say that he's asked me twice if he should shave tonight and what shirt to wear."

Smiling, he winked as he walked out of the building. She made her way up the stairs to her apartment feeling, for the moment, that everything would be okay.

****

Holly's cell rang as she put away her groceries. She accepted the call and heard the voice of her best friend Allie. "I haven't heard your voice in like a week. Are you still alive?"

She chuckled. "Didn't I text you the other day?"

"Yes, but that was about a TV show and a text isn't really talking. I just miss you."

Holly couldn't help but smile. She and Allie had met in college though the theater department. She was someone you could always count on to go out on a Friday night with you and liven up the mood. But also someone who you could confess a secret to and no judgement would come your way. If Holly needed a logical opinion, she turned to Kate, if she needed anything else, Allie was the place to go.

After a few years of living in the city with her and Kate, Allie took a job in Madison, Wisconsin and now only saw them every few months. With the world slowly reopening, a reunion between the friends kept getting rescheduled.

"I'm sorry, but I've been rather busy getting to know my new neighbor who I'm cooking for tonight."

A gasp, followed by sounds of rustling, came over the phone. "I knew it. I was reading the cards while thinking of you and saw some big things coming your way."

Over the last couple of years, Allie had developed an affinity for astrology and tarot cards—all of which meant she'd taken to reading for friends and family. Holly didn't necessarily believe in tarot, but she also didn't not believe… In her opinion, it was better to listen to opinions from all angles instead of just one, so she always welcomed a reading from her friend.

"What did the cards say about me exactly?"

"I was having a bottle of wine and just doing general readings for the family and friends because you know, it was a Wednesday night, but yours definitely stood out because I got a lot of the Major Arcana cards."

Holly had heard enough readings to understand this to mean she had pulled the cards with names like "The Tower" rather than "The 3 of Swords". Allie had pulled a lot of major life cards, intrigued, Holly asked her to elaborate.

"Remember, I don't want you to read too much into this, but I was shuffling and thinking of you and The Lovers fell out first. A partnership will form."

Holly immediately thought of Luke. Clearly, they had formed this investigative partnership, but her asking him on a date tonight could be the beginning of a romantic one.

Allie continued. "Then quickly after that, two cards fell out at the same time: the King of Swords and The Tower. You're going to get some mental clarity, some truth and then…well obviously this can be taken in a few ways but how it popped into my head was that something was going to basically blow up and come to an end. That does not necessarily have to do with the first card, but I think it's tied in with finding the truth. I think basically the King of Swords will lead you to the Tower."

Holly was silent; would she find out a disturbing truth about Luke? Finding out the truth… Something niggled in the back of her mind, maybe finding something out about Phil. She did have the encounter with him earlier that day, maybe she would find out the truth about the scarf.

"Holly? You still there?"

Deep in thought, she forgot that Allie was still on the line. "Yes. I'm sorry. I was just…that is a lot to think about."

"Oh jeez. I hope I didn't freak you out or anything. Seriously do not put too much stock into these things, the future can always change. Forget all that and give me some updates on you, tell me about this neighbor. Have you touched lips yet?"

Holly laughed at the abrupt change of subject. "We actually have, but it was not…I mean…it wasn't a romantic thing but also it was so good."

Squeals of excitement rang out. "If it was that good, that means maybe you'll have a little more tonight. A little kissing, maybe a cocktail…"

As she trailed off, Holly said, "I didn't plan on drinking cocktails. I have wine for dinner so—"

Allie cut her off. "Not the kind you drink. I meant it as, you know, a cock-tail." Waiting until Holly understood the euphemism, she immediately burst into laughter.

"No one calls that a cocktail," she said laughing.

Allie giggled. "They will now."

Holly let the worrisome thoughts drift to the back of her mind as she filled in her friend on the rest of the gossip of her past week. They spoke for another half hour, ending the call with her promises to fill her friend in on all the details of the night to come, including if she ended up drinking a cocktail.

****

As the time drew near, Holly began prepping the meal. Turning on her cooking playlist, or the old crooners as Kate called it, she started grabbing ingredients. Cooking was something she enjoyed; she found it relaxing and gratifying. Most of the time anyway. She wasn't a professional chef by any means. To enjoy her creations with friends was a simple pleasure for her. She was touched when Luke had created the meal he had for her, it wasn't just reheated food but something he had put thought and time into, it made her feel like he cared. She wanted to return the favor, return the feelings in her dish.

She was never into cooking growing up; that was her father's area of expertise. She was always off at rehearsals or practices and would come home to find a delicious meal on the table. Before heading off to college she realized that the school-provided meal plan only sounded good, so she started watching her dad prepare food when she came home for the odd weekend. He taught her how to trust her eye when it came to seasoning, how to use any leftover vegetables in any dish, how to use the most random kitchen instrument. In learning all this, she understood that cooking was not about the anxiety of getting a meal on the table in time, it was about taking the time to create something that not only you but others could enjoy as well.

After creating the creamy white sauce and seasoning the chicken, she placed the cutlets into a frying pan to blacken both sides. When that was done, she placed everything into the oven to cook. She'd wait for Luke to arrive before cooking the pasta as that would take the least amount of time.

Once that was underway, she went into her room to change. She opted for a navy-blue jumpsuit with spaghetti straps. It wasn't too fancy but not too casual either and, if she was going to be sitting on her couch all night, she wanted to be comfortable but still cute. She threw up half of her hair into a low bun and put on some small silver hoops.

She looked at the clock: five forty-five, and ran around relighting a few candles from earlier for ambiance. Holly grabbed two glasses and uncorked the wine, giggling slightly thinking back to her conversation with Allie, when there was a knock on her door.

Opening the door, she found Luke standing there, looking devastating in black jeans and a gray T-shirt with a light-blue button up shirt layered over it, he'd rolled up the sleeves to reveal a set of ripped forearms. A black leather-strapped watch adorned his left wrist and in his right hand he held a package of cookies. She realized she was holding her breath, too excited by his presence to remember that she needed oxygen to live. She let it all out in a whoosh and gave a nervous chuckle.

He stood there, smile on his face, and waving a package in his right hand. "I was brought up on the 'always bring something to someone's house' rule so I figured I would go for dessert."

As she stepped aside to let him through the doorway, she caught a whiff of his cologne. The scent made her knees weak and in trying not to show how much he affected her, she said in an upbeat tone, "I was also raised on that rule, and it is very much appreciated."

She watched as he walked into the main room, taking in his surroundings as if he hadn't stood right there just yesterday. He did not look out of place as he placed down the cookies and sat comfortably on the couch. He leaned over and clapped his hands together. "Is there anything I can help with?"

Handing him a glass, she replied, "Nope. All I need to do is cook the pasta, and that only takes a few minutes.

Pour the wine and relax. I'll be in and out."

She walked into the kitchen and placed her hands on the counter, closed her eyes, and took a breath. She had to calm down, just because he was beautiful and smelled so good and his forearms were sexy... *Oh dear God I'm even attracted to his forearms, what is wrong with me?* she thought as she dumped the box of pasta into the waiting boiling water. She needed to get a grip and have a nice, normal night instead of jumping his bones. The playlist was still playing, and Rosemary Clooney's voice filled the space, Holly started to sway to the music, relaxing herself and stirring the noodles.

"Sorry to interrupt the dance party but, uh, is the wine in here?"

She jumped and turned as Luke enter the kitchen. He looked up into space, his face fixed into concentration and asked, "I know this song I think?"

She gripped the countertop tightly to stop herself from reaching out to him and let out a breath she had not realized she was holding in. "Um yeah, I like this kind of stuff when I cook. It's not too crazy that I'll spill food, but it's not too boring, so that I'll fall asleep and burn myself or something."

"Well don't let me stop you, I won't let you dance alone." He started to sway but couldn't find the beat of the song. She giggled then grabbed his hands to slow him down and sway him to the correct beat. He smiled a goofy smile and she felt herself mirror him.

Then she remembered he asked about wine. "Oh jeez I forgot." She dropped his hands and spun around reaching for the bottle. "The wine is right here."

She watched as he came closer and leaned over to grab the bottle. She looked up into his sparkling green eyes which were boring into hers.

His voice lowered, the tone becoming huskier. "It smells really good in here. Whatever you're making is going to be delicious." He paused a moment, letting the tension hang in the air. He broke the spell and looked down at the bottle then back to her, he cleared his throat. "Let me go pour this."

"Yeah, good idea, I'll be out in a moment if you want to take them to the table?"

After he left the confines of the kitchen, she relaxed and poured the sauce over the cooked pasta, cut the chicken into strips, then plated it all and brought it out to him.

After one bite, his eyes went wide. "This is amazing."

Feeling anxiety and nerves drift away, Holly dug in.

Conversation flowed easily between them, they chatted about what movies and shows they had recently been binging. She was happy to hear they liked the same sitcoms although he confessed to never having watched any of the crime procedurals that she was obsessed with, but she could forgive him for that. As he went on about shows she started to picture the two of them curled up on the couch, watching them together, his arm around her, she cuddled into him. She liked that idea, it felt natural, maybe she could maneuver that later.

"So" he continued, "Tommy mentioned that he quite literally ran into you and said you looked a bit frazzled. What happened?"

Holly considered a moment not telling him about her encounter with Second Window, about lying and blaming it on her 'to do list', but she decided against it. He had been with her through this whole journey, and he should probably be up to date on things.

She started out slowly, fortified with a sip of wine, "I was on my way to the store today and I met Phil."

"Phil?"

"Yeah, that is Second Window Man's real name."

Suddenly, he looked up from his plate with a look on his face that was so fierce, she sat back in her chair. Speaking loud and fast, he demanded, "He came up to you? Did he threaten you? Jesus, Hol."

He leaned back and ran a hand through his hair. At the same time, he closed his eyes and took a deep breath. When he opened them, he looked at her more calmly and reached grabbing her hands with his on top of the table. "Most importantly, are you okay?" His green eyes searched her face as if looking for any signs of damage.

She took a shaky breath before she responded. "I'm fine now. I wasn't at the time though." She relayed the whole experience to Luke who sat there listening intently, never letting go of her hands.

Once she had finished the story, anger still burned in Luke's eyes. "I'm calling the police again."

He made movements to get up and she tugged his hands, putting him back into his seat. "Don't you think I thought about that? He didn't do anything, he didn't threaten me directly, and I don't want to call the police at every little thing and have them write me off as some scared little girl. They already didn't find anything in his home."

Frustrated, she collected the plates and headed into the kitchen. She dumped them into the sink as well as all the pots and pans she had used.

"Hol?"

She turned and Luke was standing in the entryway

to the kitchen, her glass of wine refilled in his hand. "I'm sorry that happened."

She took the glass from him and took a big swig. Placing it on the counter, she immediately wrapped her arms around his waist. Without wasting a moment, his arms covered her in his warm embrace. It seemed like they fit together like this, his body contoured to hers and created a perfect nook for her to lean into. His hand lay gently in between her shoulder blades, running slowly up and down. Her head was level with his collarbone, and she inhaled his scent. Plus, hearing the steady beat of his heart relaxed her.

She did not know how much time had passed or how long they stood this way. She slowly tilted up her head to meet his eyes. Their lips were so close. She could see his eyes flick back and forth from her eyes to her mouth and back again. He must be thinking the same thing, that if she just stood up on her tiptoes just a little bit and he leaned down…

A loud crash came from outside the back door, and the spell was broken. They both looked in the direction of the sound and Luke tightened his hold on her, in a more protective gesture.

"What was that?"

Chapter Nine

Holly pulled away from Luke's comforting embrace and went to the back door. Cracking it open, she saw nothing out of place. Confused, she turned to him when another loud crash rang out. Moving right behind her, he opened the door wider. Together, they stuck their heads out, looking into the alleyway. Holly forced herself to concentrate on the noise and not the heat radiating up and down her back from Luke's body.

The crashing, they realized, was coming from Phil's bedroom. They were able to see him, on the phone, pacing back and forth in his room. He looked angry and seemed to be yelling into the receiver, but they couldn't make out what he was saying. He paused and then, apparently angry at what he heard, kicked something on the floor of his room.

Luke murmured, "I wonder what the bad news is."

Phil ended his call and left the room, turning the light off. The faint glow of the rest of the apartment disappeared from view as well.

Holly leaned back inside and pulled Luke with her. "We need to follow him."

He looked at her as if she had just grown another head. "Follow him? We should not go anywhere near that man."

Holly raced to the front of her apartment and began to put on her sandals. "We need to see where he's going.

What if he leads us to some sort of evidence we can tell, or better yet show, the police." She grabbed a dark hoodie. "Look, if he gets on the 'L' we won't follow him. If it's somewhere close, don't you want to at least try? We can pretend we're just out for a walk."

Reluctantly he agreed and they raced out the door slowing down at the corner of the building. They waited for a few moments before they saw Phil leave his building. He had put on a worn blue baseball hat and a light jacket. Shoving his hands in his pockets, he turned left and started walking at a quick pace. Letting him get a head start, Luke then grabbed her hand and started walking in the same direction.

They kept what they deemed a safe distance between Phil and them. He was far enough that they could not quite make out his features, figuring that he, in turn, would not be able to tell it was them, but close enough that they didn't lose sight of his blue hat. There were a few people out that night, but not so many that they would mistake him for anyone else.

Phil took a left at the end of their street and onto a main road. After following him for about ten minutes, he stopped in front of a big building on the corner and went inside. As they got closer to the building, Holly felt excitement bubbling in her chest. Maybe this was where he kept his kidnapped victims or maybe a second home? Reaching the front, they looked up and saw it was a storage facility and no one was in the lobby. Luke tried the door, it was unlocked. He stopped and asked, "Are you sure we should do this?"

Holly nodded, and they cautiously tiptoed inside. The lobby was a small beige room with an unoccupied desk and to the left was a door with a small window.

Luke peered through the window whispering, "I see him. We can't go through yet."

The small window was just high enough that she was unable to peek through, so Luke was left to continue narrating what he saw.

"Okay he has a key and is unlocking his unit. He's pulling up the door and he's inside." He remained silent for several seconds, then said, "Okay the door is still open and a light went on."

After five minutes Phil had not reappeared. They decided to leave and wait outside on the corner of the block to watch when he left. After fifteen minutes, he came through the doors rubbing his hands. He turned and started walking back the way he came.

She held Luke back from following. "Let's go inside and see if there is anything around the door."

The two walked in and after looking through the small window again to confirm no one was there, went through. Inside was a gray hallway lined with bright orange garage-style doors, they walked down the hall and stopped in front of the one Phil had stood outside and inspected everything.

Holly was sure something would have fallen out from the unit, a slip of paper that he had forgotten to tuck away which got blown out of the door or there would be scratches, anything. She examined the door, kneeling to look at the padlock and gave it a tug to see if it would give, which it did not. She even put her ear to the door, hoping she would hear a missing girl on the other side scream for help, but was met with silence. Once they concluded that nothing was out of order, they exited the building and made their way back home.

She looped her arm through Luke's as they slowly

walked down the street. "I'm sorry for dragging you out. I was so sure…" She trailed off, partly lost in her thoughts but also embarrassed.

He nudged her, his green eyes encouraging her to continue. "Sure of what?"

"Sure of finding something like in the movies and TV. And I know life isn't like that, but my life has really been feeling like an episode of some crime drama recently. I was sort of hoping the girls were alive and that's where he was keeping them or something." She looked down at her feet. "I swear this isn't what I normally do on dates," she forced a short laugh, "I hope uh…you don't think I'm…I don't even know."

"I wouldn't laugh at you for something like this if that's what you're afraid of." He looked down at her, his features serious. "Remember I've seen everything you have too. I believe you and I'm not letting you do anything involving him alone. The next time you see him you call me immediately."

As they got nearer to their building, a figure came into view. It was someone leaning against the neighboring building, smoking a cigarette and wearing a blue hat. Phil. The mood shifted once more.

"Luke…" She tightened her grip on his arm. Tilting her head down, she pulled up her hood and slowed her step so that she was almost blocked by his body.

"It's okay," he said under his breath. "Keep walking."

As they walked past him, Phil looked up, glancing at the couple. Luke looked straight ahead, guiding Holly around the corner of their building. Taking longer strides he caused her to speed walk in order to keep pace. Quickly, he opened the door and practically pushed her through, taking only a moment to look over his shoulder before following her inside.

At her apartment door, she turned as if to say goodnight when Luke, slightly tense, said, "I'm going to come in if that's all right." Attempting to lighten the mood he added, "We haven't had dessert yet." He gave her a small smile that made her heart flutter.

Her hand, slightly shaking, stilled a little as relief flooded her body, she was not prepared to be alone quite yet. After a few attempts, she got the key in the lock, letting them inside.

Silently, she kicked off her shoes, shrugged off the hoodie, and walked into the kitchen to grab her forgotten glass of wine. She sat on the couch as Luke did the same, scooping up the cookies as well. He stretched his arm over the back of the couch giving her the opportunity to lean into him.

This was what she imagined for the night. Cuddling on the couch. Except in that fantasy, they were watching something and probably making out. Not like this, being scared out of her mind. "Did he watch us when we came in here?"

He took a deep breath, her head rose and fell with his chest. "He didn't follow us or look around the corner, but he did turn his head and watch when we walked by."

Holly turned her face and burrowed into the crook of his neck.

Luke continued; his voice sounded muffled with her head buried. "If it's okay with you, I'd like to sleep on your couch tonight. I mean…if that's all right. I really do not like the idea that you'll be alone tonight. I promise I'll be gone before you wake up."

She lifted her head from his chest. "You really don't

have to do th—"

She was cut off suddenly as his head bent down and he captured her lips with his. After a moment, he pulled back and hesitated—then she grabbed the collar of his shirt and yanked him back down.

This was not like their first kiss. That one surprised her and was slow and sweet with just a hint of passion. This was hard and fast. Holly felt the emotion behind it. She could taste his hunger as it matched her own. Her hands flew to his head, entwining her fingers in his curls. She pulled him closer wanting to deepen the kiss.

Following her lead, he let himself be led on top of her until they were fully lying on the couch with his body covering hers. His right hand moved toward her rib cage as he used his left hand to hold his weight as to not crush her. He angled his head, opening his mouth, making Holly's face tilt up. She lifted and tangled her legs around his as their kisses became more frantic. All the stress, fear, and anger melted away leaving her with the arousal that had been building between them since the previous night. She wanted him, she wanted him badly.

His mouth left hers and moved to her neck. The kisses on her lips had been hard and fast, but now he teased her with light licks and grazing teeth. She gasped, her breathing became fast, and she did not want him to stop. His mouth moved back up to hers as his right hand cupped her breasts through the thin fabric and started massaging. Holly felt a zing of pleasure as he lightly pinched her budded nipples. She arched her chest up, filling his large palm with the rest of her breast. His hand began to slide down to her waist and began to search for an opening. She forgot she was wearing a jumpsuit and that the top was indeed attached to the bottom.

Realizing what he was trying to do made Holly begin to giggle. Luke pulled back and looked down in confusion. Realization dawned on him as to why he was not able to put his hand where he wanted. Laughing with her, he slowly eased himself up to a sitting position, pulling her with him.

Taking a moment to compose themselves, Luke spoke first. "I'm sorry. I didn't mean to... I don't want you to think that I want to stay here because I want to—er—I mean I don't not want that, but I don't want to do anything you don't." He blew out a frustrated sigh, running his hand through his hair. He looked adorable.

"Don't worry, I know what you mean." She walked to her room, coming out a moment later with a pillow. "I think you're a good guy and, while I really wish I wasn't wearing a jumpsuit right now, I think maybe our emotions are running high and we just got caught up in the moment." Walking to the other side of the living room, she grabbed a few blankets.

"Why don't you run home and grab some pajamas while I clean up?"

"No need, I usually sleep in my boxers and a T-shirt. Why don't you go get ready and let me clean up? It's the least I can do since you cooked."

She gladly accepted and moved into her room to change and try to cool off. Briefly she considered changing into her lingerie and coming out of her room as a surprise. She could run out there right now and pull him to her, knowing that he would not say no, but she couldn't. Not with Phil still in her mind. She needed to keep her head clear and her pants on.

Changing quickly, she cautiously opened the door to hear water running. He was still washing dishes and she took the opportunity to use the bathroom. She emerged to find him in the living room, done cleaning up in the kitchen…and taking off his jeans. Holly was in shock, her eyes were drawn to that first feature of his she ever saw, now encased only in briefs, which really accentuated just how perfect his ass really was. Realizing this was bordering on creepy, she found her voice.

"Oh I'm sorry, I wasn't expecting dinner and a show."

He instantly pulled his pants back up and turned around, a blush spreading across his cheeks. "I'm sorry. I just thought you were in bed."

She walked toward him, her shyness creeping in. "It's still kind of early for me, would you want to hang out, maybe watch TV?"

Nodding in agreement, the two curled up on the couch. It was a perfect ending, Holly thought, to one of the best and possibly weirdest dates ever.

Chapter Ten

Luke woke with a sore neck and a smile on his face. The neck pain was definitely from using the armrest of the couch as a pillow. The smile could be explained by waking up with Holly still on top of him. She had fallen asleep in the middle of the show last night. He'd not wanted to wake her, mostly because she looked so peaceful, but another part of him wanted to be near her all night.

She was still asleep, her head on his abdomen, thankfully she wasn't a drooler. He grabbed a discarded pillow from the ground and tried to ease her head onto it while moving out of the way. Mumbling, she shifted onto her new pillow but was able to stay asleep while being transferred.

He got up and stretched, heading to the bathroom as he thought about the night before. He wasn't able to stop himself from kissing her when she had looked up at him with those wide blue eyes. If it wasn't for her clothing, he probably would not have been able to stop himself on that couch either.

He thought about the way she felt last night, her skin just as soft as he had imagined. He hoped Holly didn't notice that he needed to stay seated for a bit once she had gotten up. The evidence of his arousal would have been clear as day. Just thinking about her now he could feel himself getting excited again.

He checked the time and realized it was still early enough that he should let her sleep in after the excitement of last night. In the meantime, he would try and make her some breakfast. He headed into the kitchen to see what he could use and found pancake mix and coffee and got to work.

As he flipped the last pancake, he heard movement in the other room. She shuffled into the kitchen, eyes still half closed. Her curly hair was messed up; her oversized shirt hung off one shoulder with her tiny shorts just peeking out from underneath; and she looked utterly adorable. Luke had to stop himself from taking her in his arms and kissing her right then and there. Instead, he poured a cup of coffee and placed it in her hand. He knew the second the smell hit her. Her eyes opened all the way then came to life.

"So what do we have here?" she asked, her voice raspy from sleep.

"I, uh, made pancakes for you. I hope that's okay?"

She smiled. "I think that's perfect, thank you."

After plating everything, he carried the food to the table and watched as she took a bite.

"Oh my goodness, these are so good. They never taste as good when I make them."

Luke was warmed by her praise. "Thank you. I like to add some vanilla and cinnamon to the generic mix, makes it taste better. So, what are your plans today?"

She thought for a moment while chewing. "Honestly, I have nothing to do. I was going to clean but then this guy came over last night and decided to be wonderful and clean everything for me. Other than wait for Kate to come home tomorrow morning, I got nothing."

"I haven't really walked to the lakefront in a long time. Would you want to join me?"

Her eyes lit up at the suggestion. "I'd love to. Why don't we meet outside around noon? That way we have time to shower and stuff?"

The picture of them showering together came instantly. Just as quickly, he banished it. "Yes, that sounds good." His voice a bit rougher than he meant; he just hoped Holly didn't notice the effect she had on him.

After they finished breakfast, Holly scooped up the plates. "No please," he protested, "I made a mess in the kitchen. Let me clean it."

She answered him by bending down and giving him a small, quick kiss on the lips which took him by surprise. "Go home and shower," she said. "I'll see you in a few hours."

Luke grabbed the plates out of her hand and put them down as he turned and kissed Holly again. He started slowly, gently using his tongue to open her lips. She tasted sweet like syrup.

I could kiss her all day.

Her hands landed softly on his forearms and slid up, hooking behind his neck. His arms circled her waist and pulled her closer. Her chest pressed up against him, and he could feel the curve of her through the thin sleep shirt. He started to become aroused. He desperately wanted to lead her to her bedroom and discover what was under that T-shirt, but he knew he shouldn't. He reluctantly began to pull away, peppering her lips with soft kisses.

"So, I guess I'll be going now."

"You should really leave more often if that's how you say goodbye." She slowly released her hands from the back of his neck and backed away.

She ran her fingers through her hair and Luke noticed her shirt pull against her chest, giving him a clear view of her budded nipples. He swallowed hard, averting his gaze before he had difficulty walking again.

"I'll see you in a few hours then." With a smile, he turned and left her apartment, walking across the hall into his own.

Tommy looked up from his place on the couch. "Well, well, well, where have you been all night long? And in the same clothes, too…"

Luke sat next to his roommate. His head rolled back onto the couch back and he exhaled loudly, certain he was wearing the dumbest of dumb smiles on his face.

Tommy angled, smacking him on the arm. "I've been cooped up writing cover letters and resumes, so I need to hear some serious details."

"Nothing happened, at least not what you're thinking. I can honestly say it was a date unlike any other. She is so… I mean…" He suddenly turned to him in accusation. "How come you've never introduced us before?"

His friend's hands went up in defense. "Hey, it's not like her and I were best friends. We've just worked together. And you have never asked me to set you up. I have been telling you about single girls I know for years, and you always blow me off. You have always seemed happy to be alone, you venture out when you want, and you stay at home when you want."

"I would've ventured out a lot sooner if I had known about her. I mean she's just…she's great."

Tommy angled back to the TV. "I thought you were gonna say you were in love, ha."

Luke looked at his friend a moment longer. "When

was the last time you worked on a stand-up set? Or maybe wrote like a sketch or something?"

"Before the move. I've got to put that stuff on the backburner and find a day job right now."

Luke smiled sympathetically. "I admire the drive but...make sure you're still doing what you love."

He filled him in on his plans for the rest of the day and got up to get in the shower. As he stepped in, he thought about what Tommy said: he'd never been in love before or didn't think he had. But nothing had ever felt like this did. Maybe this was love at first sight; it had only been a few weeks, but he could not stop thinking about Holly. He wanted to be around her all the time, he wanted to talk to her about everything, and he wanted to just touch her. The question was, did she feel the same or was she someone who was more casual?

The weather channel reported that it would be hot today. Luke wore basketball shorts and a white T-shirt. With some time to kill before seeing Holly, he went in the kitchen to make some lunch. The smell of an overflowing trash can hit him before he got fully in the room. Annoyed with his friend, he grabbed the bag and headed out the back to the dumpster.

He opened the gate that stood between the alley and the parking area where the dumpsters for the entire block were lined up in a semi-neat row. From the corner of one eye he saw movement.

Looking closer, he found Phil throwing something into one of the dumpsters. Turning toward him, he smiled and put a hand up to wave.

Luke paused for a moment before doing the same. Moving slowly, he took his time to toss the bag away, waiting until Phil turned and walked back through his gate and out of sight. When he was unable to hear his footsteps echoing through the alley, Luke walked over to Phil's dumpster and opened it. He did not have a desire to go through the trash but seeing as he and Holly already followed the guy to a storage locker the night before, he felt like he should at least take a peek. Grabbing the closed bag on top of the pile in the dumpster, he hefted it to the ground.

Making sure no one was watching, he turned the bag on its side and shook out the contents. Empty yogurt cups, tissues, plastic wrappings. He shook out a bit more, food scraps, aluminum foil, paper towels with rust on it…he went back to the last item and kicked it around with his shoe. Dried blood was rust colored. He gave the bag one more shake, now dumping it all on the ground and saw a torn, balled up, flannel shirt, also with rust-colored stains.

Immediately Luke took out his phone and snapped a photo of the contents now splayed on the ground. He looked around for something to pick up the shirt with, finding a discarded plastic bag balled up behind the dumpster. Being careful not to touch the fabric, he grabbed the shirt through the plastic, wrapping it in the bag. Luke tightened the now half full trash bag and tossed it back into the dumpster. Trying to make it look like an animal got into the dumpster, he kicked around the trash that was already scattered on the ground.

He hurried back into his apartment, bag in hand and ran through to the front. He decided it was better to take the long way to her, limiting the possibility of Phil seeing him with his discarded shirt. After banging on Holly's door, he waited impatiently.

She answered wearing only a short silky robe and

wet from the shower. What started out as a lazy smile vanished instantly. "What happened? Are you okay?"

She motioned for him to come in, and he hurriedly closed and locked the door behind him. Walking into the main room, he turned to see her following with a concerned look on her face. Normally, he would have taken the time to think about what exactly she looked like underneath that silky robe, but he was too worked up.

"I did something a little weird. I was throwing out my trash at the same time as Phil. When he went back in, I decided to look through it a little just to see...um...well what he was throwing away."

He paused, waiting for her to recoil in disgust or chastise him. Instead, she looked eager for him to continue and waved her hand to tell him to keep going.

Emboldened he went on, "I didn't touch anything except the trash bag, and I shook some of it out on the street and I saw some paper towels and they seemed to be blood stained."

Holly's eyes went wide. "Did you grab them? Did you take a picture?"

"I would've if I didn't find something better." He grinned, producing the plastic bag to let her peer into. "It's one of his shirts. It's torn and bloodstained." At this she gasped and leaned away from the bag with a look of disbelief.

"Oh my God, we have evidence now. We can call the cops." Holly shot up, arms raised above her head in a victorious pose.

Luke stood and tossed the bag on the coffee table. He wrapped his arms around her and picked her up, swinging her in a tight circle. Laughing, they stopped moving and looked at each other, Holly now at eye level raised up in his arms. The tension between them was thick. Acutely aware that the silky robe had hiked up, Luke felt part of her thigh in his hand. He swallowed hard and she smirked with eyebrow raised. Before he could speak, she bent her head down, connecting their mouths.

He inhaled her scent as her wet hair lightly tickled his cheek. Her hands were on either side of his head, tilting it, making the kiss deeper.

Thank God I went with basketball shorts, he thought as he felt his arousal grow.

"Did you want to see my bedroom?"

Carrying her into the bedroom, Luke kicked the door shut behind him. He placed her on the bed and followed, positioning himself on top of her. The shift caused her robe to gape open, exposing the valley between her breasts. Unable to take his eyes off it, he touched the silky hem by her neck and slowly started to trace it down. Holly's breath hitched and his eyes flicked back to hers, the desire in her eyes mirroring his own.

Leaning down, he kissed her as his fingers began to push the robe aside, exposing her left breast. He broke off the kiss moving his head down toward it and took it in his mouth. Holly gasped in pleasure and arched her back, pushing herself farther into his mouth. He took that as an okay to pull back the other side of her robe. *This woman has the most perfect chest I've ever seen.*

Giggling caused him to look up, her lips tweaked upward. "You just going to stare at them or...?"

Luke had never been issued a more enjoyable challenge and bent his head to get to work. Before he could start, however, Holly's body stiffened and she placed her hands on his shoulder, a look of confusion crossed her face.

"Do you hear that?"

Luke focused, shaking his head out of the lustful haze. At first there was nothing, then, very faintly, he heard hinges creaking at the back door.

"Did you leave your back door open?" asked Luke, eyes glued to the opening of the bedroom door.

"No."

Pulling her up from the bed and securing her robe closed, Luke led them cautiously from the bedroom. He slowly moved toward the kitchen making sure to put himself between the sound and Holly. Finally rounding the corner, they found the back door wide open and the kitchen empty.

"Does anything look out of place?" Luke asked, still firmly planted between the door and Holly.

Gripping his upper arm, Holly peered around him toward the kitchen. "I don't think so."

Luke relaxed as he walked to door, closing and securing it. "Probably a really strong gust of wind or something."

Holly stood in the middle of the kitchen, her arms wrapped around herself. He moved in to comfort her when suddenly a bang sounded from the other end of the apartment. In one stride, Luke grabbed her and roughly pushed her behind him as he moved towards the next room.

A tall figure wearing jeans and an upturned black hoodie ran out of the apartment through the front door. Luke quickly looked around, making sure no one else was with the intruder. He turned to Holly and yelled to stay and call the police as he immediately began to give chase.

Luke reached the front door of the building and flung it wide open, looking for signs of a black hoodie. He watched a blur round the corner and chased after it. As he followed, he nearly ran into an old woman with a grocery cart, stopping just before collision and apologizing he moved past and looked around. The person in the black hoodie disappeared. Turning, he jogged back to the apartment.

The cops were on their way according to Holly. He entered and without stopping he grabbed her, pulling her into a hug. He held her tight and thanked God he'd been in the apartment when all this occurred. He did not want to think what would've happened if she'd been alone.

"Has anything been damaged or stolen?"

He didn't let her go as he felt her shake her head. Slowly, he sat them down on the couch, pulled her onto his lap, and held her. His moment of peace was short lived as he looked around the room and realized that something was missing.

The bag containing the shirt was gone.

Chapter Eleven

The police arrived ten minutes after Holly's call to 911. Their response time was a tad too long for her liking but as the actual crime was already completed, and no one had been injured, she figured they assumed there was no need for a rush. It had, at least, given her time to change out of her robe into actual clothes.

She hastily pulled on a bra and shirt and feeling the fabric against her skin made her remember how Luke's mouth made her feel. Erotic thoughts were rapidly replaced by those of an unknown assailant invading her space, bringing her back to the present with a crash.

When Luke realized the bag containing the shirt was gone, it took everything Holly had to not burst into tears. It shook her, going from feeling so happy to so scared in the span of a few minutes. Her space had been violated, the evidence taken, she was afraid of what would happen next. What had she gotten the two of them into?

Luke stayed with her when Officers Shane and Martinez arrived, although she doubted he would leave her alone at this moment. Since he entered back into the apartment, he had not let her out of his sight except for when she changed. Even then, he stood outside her bedroom door.

After entering, the officers walked around, surveying the apartment. They pointed out the locks on both doors had been picked, not broken. Officer Shane had them both sit on the couch while Martinez examined the lock.

"Let's start from the beginning," Shane said.

His calm demeanor reminded Holly of her father. She would guess his age to be mid to late forties. He wore his hair buzzed short, making it easy to picture him serving in the military. His large build looked bulky with the addition of the vest he wore over his uniform.

His partner, Officer Martinez, was a visual contrast. He was a short, muscular, maybe thirty-year-old Latino. While Shane gave her the impression of a protective father, Martinez was the good-looking guy who would seduce his daughter.

Taking a breath, she began her story. She told Shane about her and Luke looking through Phil's window and about the scarf. She told him about calling in the tip and about her encounter with Phil on the street. How they followed him the night before. When she trailed off, Luke continued on, relating the events of the afternoon, finding the shirt, chasing after the intruder.

Officer Shane listened silently and looked up, finishing his final notes. "That is a lot of information. Miss Harrison, you definitely should not have followed this man, and please refrain from doing so in the future." He gave a pointed look to Holly who raised an eyebrow but did not look away.

Shane continued with his remarks. "Now about this shirt, while it is not against the law to go through trash, you have no way of knowing if this actually belonged to him and if it did, that it wasn't, in fact, his own blood."

Luke became defensive. "Listen, I took a photo of it before I grabbed it and there were those paper towels outside too with the same stains. Can you collect them or test them or something?"

Shane looked at him for a minute and then gave a curt nod. While Luke sent him the photo, Holly walked over to Officer Martinez. As she approached, he closed a small black case and looked up, giving an easy smile that under different circumstances would've given Holly butterflies in her stomach. "I'm all done here."

"Did the guy leave any prints?"

Martinez shrugged his shoulders. "We got a partial. The thing is, we are so backed up it will take a while to run and then we might not even get a hit off of it. I just wouldn't want to get your hopes up."

Holly sighed and crossed her arms. Martinez gave her a sympathetic look. "The lock is fine but why don't you go buy a chain or hook and eye, something a bit harder to pick until your landlord can get you something a bit heavier duty?"

She nodded, her unease still present. "We've given you guys this…I don't know, circumstantial evidence? I just know something is going on with Phil."

Officer Martinez smirked at her use of terminology but nodded in agreement. "We'll definitely do another check up on him and—" lowering his voice so his partner wouldn't hear, said, "—I'll go around back and see if any of those paper towels are still there. Again, I don't want to get your hopes up, the same guy might've picked them up or they could've blown away."

"Thank you for believing us."

Another nod and smile graced his face. "After you buy the locks, if you need you can call us and I can come back to help you install them."

"I appreciate that, but I've already got my lock installer over there." She gestured toward Luke.

Martinez kept his warm eyes on hers. "Then we'll be in touch."

When the policemen left, she shut the door behind them and slumped against it, all her energy suddenly evaporated. Luke came and leaned against the opposite wall also looking drained. He angled his head toward her. "How are you feeling?"

"Not great if I'm being honest. I'm scared because Phil knows we're the ones who took the shirt. I'm scared that there doesn't seem to be anything we can do. I'm scared that my apartment was broken into. I know, logically, this kind of thing happens all the time but it's just…a shit storm." She sighed, feeling her eyes brim with tears; in an instant, he was by her side, pulling her into his arms.

She let the tears fall and buried her head in his chest. He stroked her hair as she wept. After she was all cried out, she pulled herself from his arms and straightened herself up.

"Okay, that's enough of that." Holly attempted a sense of aloofness. If she pretended to be okay maybe she would feel okay. "I need to go to the store and buy a latch-hook lock or whatever it's called for some extra protection."

Luke watched cautiously as she grabbed her purse. "I'll come with you."

"No." Holly paused in grabbing her things and looked at him. "I really appreciate the offer and while part of me doesn't want to be alone right now, another part needs a minute to be by myself and think things out." She continued getting ready to go but Luke reached out and grabbed her shoulders, stopping her again. "I really don't want you to be left alone. Not with him out there.

I don't want anything to happen to you."

Holly shook his hands off before moving to the door. "I really, *really* like you. And I really like that you're worried about me, but I am a grown woman. I need to clear my head, and I'm also just going to the end of the block and coming back. How about I knock on your door when I'm back, and I'll let you install this lock for me?"

They stared at each other until Luke dropped back, defeat in his body language. "Okay, but please knock on my door the minute you get back."

Holly nodded as they both exited the apartment. Luke watched from his doorway as she walked down the few steps and to the door of the building. "Please be careful."

With a small smile, she walked out the door.

****

The trip to the store at the corner of her street was uneventful except that every car horn, every random bang and generic loud noise had her jumping out of her skin. She probably looked like she was on drugs, checking over her shoulder at the slightest of noises, fidgeting and unable to focus.

She ended up buying four different locks, figuring two different ones on each door would make her feel more secure. Walking back from the store, she managed to calm herself down and think about her options. Maybe she should leave the city for a while, go visit her parents. She looked down her brownstone-lined street and anger flooded her body. She loved it here and was not going to be chased away from her home. There was also Luke, she didn't want to leave him here alone, not after she got him into this mess. She could try and take him with her, but what would she tell her parents?

Oh, here's a boy I've been on two dates with, we're lying low from our neighbor who we think kidnaps and probably kills women.

If she were to leave, Kate would be alone. Holly simply couldn't bring another person into this mess.

As she rounded the corner of her building, she caught Tommy on his way out. "Holly. Are you okay? I caught some of the news from Luke."

She shrugged and gave a half-hearted nod, putting on a brave face. "I—" Her voice broke and she had to stop in an attempt to calm herself.

Concerned, Tommy gently led her toward the stoop. "Sit with me for a minute."

She sat and put her head in her hands, not speaking. Thankfully, he didn't push, but placed a reassuring hand on her back. After a few minutes she said, "I hope you don't resent me for getting Luke involved in this."

"You're dumb if you think he is anything but crazy about you. He said it himself. You've only been on two dates and he's digging through trash for you. As for me? Well, you and I are theater people so I already know how dramatic your life can be." He looked her dead in the eye, his expression serious, earning a laugh out of her. "Ah see, I knew you still had some chuckles in you."

Holly leaned in placing her head on his shoulder, and he gave her a one-armed squeeze. "Thank you for that." Feeling less guilty, she grabbed her bags and rose.

"Anytime you need a dumb joke, I am here for you." He stood up and brushed off the seat of his pants. "How about you come over and the three of us can watch a movie if you feel up to it. And our couch is very comfy if you want to spend the night, you know that, or Luke's bed of course."

"That's a very sweet offer, and I'll take it into consideration. I'll see you later." Feeling a bit lighter, she opened the door and made her way up to her apartment.

Chapter Twelve

As soon as she got back from the store, exhaustion took over and, as soon as she sat down, immediately dozed off. Pounding on her front door woke her. The panicked knocking continued as she jumped up from the couch and ran to answer it.

Luke, looking distressed, stood on the other side. "You told me you would knock on my door the moment you got back." His tone softened as she sleepily rubbed her eyes. "I was worried..."

She looked down, slightly embarrassed. "I know, I'm sorry. I ended up sitting down for a moment and I just kind of passed out, I'm just so tired."

Luke moved closer, rubbing her arm. "I'm sorry, I know I just...was...worried..." he finished lamely, looking at his feet.

"Why don't you help me put all these locks on the doors?" With a sleepy smile, she took his hand in hers and pulled him inside. He gave her a quick hug and a kiss on top of her head. Inhaling his scent, she felt a tug in her stomach and quickly letting him go.

For the next hour, they proceeded to install four different locks on her two separate doors. They worked well for the most part. Luke calmed her when she yelled in frustration at installing the third lock upside down. The whole time he was there for her, and Holly could not contain her gratitude. She didn't know how she would be handling all of this without him there. She could not believe that he hadn't gone running at the first instance of trouble, at seeing Phil with the scarf, at her blabbering on about a true crime blog.

In addition to all that, he seemed to still want her. She felt his desire when he kissed her goodbye that morning after breakfast and on the couch the night before. She wanted to believe it was because he liked her and had developed real feelings, but a small voice in the back of her mind kept playing devil's advocate. It was telling her that this was all due to the adrenaline of the situation. She would ignore the voice for now and believe what she wanted to because, she realized, she needed to right now. If she let go of that thought, that hope, she would break under the pressure of this situation.

It was around four o'clock before the installation was complete. Holly's stomach was rumbling, having not eaten since the pancakes that morning. Luke echoed Tommy's earlier suggestion that they go to his apartment and order a pizza. She hesitated until he recommended that she spend some time away from her apartment.

"It might help just to get away for a moment, even if it's only across the hall. Plus, I'll buy you a whole pizza."

She happily agreed, eagerly leading the way across the hall much to Luke's amusement.

While ordering food in the next room, Holly sat on the couch and decided it was finally time to give Kate a call. She could not put off updating her any longer about recent events.

"Hey, girl. What's going on?" Her friend picked up on the third ring, sounding happy and carefree. Instant guilt filled her, knowing the news would ruin her mood.

"Hey." She paused for a moment, then said, "So, um, how's Ben?"

Kate replied with a hint of suspicion in her voice. "He's good. It's so good to see him. What's wrong?"

"What do you mean what's wrong?"

"I know that voice, what is going on?"

Holly spoke fast, the words spilling out of her mouth. "Listen, things have escalated a tad. Basically, our apartment was broken into but don't worry because we've called the police and they came and I bought a few locks so now we have extra security. I haven't been alone, Luke has been here the whole time and I think maybe it would be good if you extended your trip for like a few days."

She could not recall the last time Kate's voice had hit this high a decibel. "Are you joking me? Are you okay? Oh my God. Is a killer after you now?"

The stream of screaming questions continued, and Holly waited until she heard a pause for breath to break back into the conversation. "Kate, please listen to me. I am completely safe and so are you. I just think it would make you feel better to extend your visit for a few days. Listen, I will send you money to pay for the hotel because—" She stopped as she began to choke up. "—because this is all my fault and I'm so sorry."

Emotion flooded the voice on the other end. "I'm scared for you."

"I know, and I'm so sorry." Tears spilled down her cheeks and onto Luke's couch. "Please forgive me. I promise everything will be okay. I'm okay."

"Of course, I forgive you, I'm just..." She sighed again. "Listen, I was going to come back tomorrow morning, but I'll wait and come back Wednesday night."

Holly sent up a silent prayer of thanks. "Okay, and I am sending you money for the hotel. Thank you for extending your trip. I'll see you in a few days."

After she got off the phone, she rested her head in her hands, trying to calm herself. Hearing Kate's voice on the other end of the phone brought up emotions she had been trying to keep under control. The guilt of putting not only herself and Luke in danger was already at a high level but now adding Kate and...

Holly shot up and ran to Luke, who was walking back into the room. "We need to get Tommy out of here."

Luke looked at her like she was crazy. "Uh Holly, Tommy isn't home right now, remember? You actually saw him—"

Her hands waved frantically, cutting him off. "No, I mean I just called Kate and told her to extend her trip for a day or two, and I think we should tell Tommy to go home and visit family or something. I just don't want anything to happen to anyone, I couldn't— I can't—" Emotion started to overcome her once again.

Luke put a comforting arm around her and shushed her. "I know. I couldn't either. You're right, that would actually be a good idea. We'll talk to him when he gets home."

"You might want to think about going—"

"None of that now," he said, cutting her off. "I'm perfectly happy staying here. Now come here." He led her back to the couch and put on a funny movie to help take their minds off recent events. Soon the pizza was there, and arriving right after was Tommy.

Enthusiasm filled the room as he entered with a big smile on his face. "You guys will never guess what happened to me today. I got a job!"

Luke shot up and gave Tommy a hug and slap on the back while Holly raised her one hand in celebration, the other was busy shoving a slice of pizza into her mouth.

"I know, I know, I start next week. It's a customer service position, but people pleasing is my specialty so I'm not mad." He turned to Luke. "Now don't get mad because I know we just moved in, but I think I'm actually going to go visit my parents before the job starts. Plus," he lowered his voice to a stage whisper so Holly could still hear, "it will give you a chance to have alone time with the lady."

Holly snorted with laughter as Luke rolled his eyes. "I'm ignoring that last part but congrats, buddy. I'm so proud of you. And I think that is a great idea, stay the week, longer even. In fact, you don't need to come back, just send me money for the rent every month."

The rest of the night was filled with laughter and fun, almost like a crazy man wasn't on their trail. Holly felt genuinely happy in what might have been the first time in a long time.

Luke suggested that she stay over and offered up his bed, earning a grin from Tommy. While she declined the offer of the bed, she did decide to stay the night on the couch.

Heading back across the hall to change, she ruminated on her situation. Under normal circumstances, sleeping at a man's house would lead her to choose a cute matching set of pajamas, possibly throw on mascara for that "natural" look, but she just didn't have it in her right now. Tonight, she needed comfort, which meant a pair of old gym shorts and an oversized Blackhawks T-shirt. Finally she headed back across the hall and curled up on the couch, eyes closed, ready to pass out. The sound of footsteps made their way into the room, stopping next to her. She opened her eyes to find Luke in the reclining chair next to the couch. She raised an eyebrow in question.

"You've had a long day and you're sleeping on a couch in a new place. I figured I'd hang out here until you fell asleep." He closed his eyes and leaned his head back, signaling this was non-negotiable. The last thing she saw before sleep took her was a small smile on Luke's face. Warm, fuzzy feelings spread through her as she drifted off.

****

Luke awoke for the second day in a row with a sore body. He had slept the whole night on the chair next to Holly who still lay sleeping. Part of him felt silly for not getting up and going to his own bed. She was a grown woman who didn't need a babysitter. The other part of him, however, kept imagining the intruder. Phil in a black hoodie, breaking in and kidnapping her, all while he slept soundly in his bed.

He got up as quietly as he could with a stiff back and went to his room instantly feeling better as the mattress squeaked under his weight. He closed his eyes thinking he would just rest until he heard her get up…

The mattress bent as extra pressure was applied. He opened his eyes to see Holly's smiling face looking down at him. His heart did a little flip. How did she manage to look so beautiful after waking up? Her curls framed her face, with strands hanging in front of her right eye; that piece fell just to her cheek where her summer freckles were peeking out. Her blue eyes crinkled as his eyes managed to focus on her, her smile growing wider.

"Good morning. I was wondering if maybe around lunch time you and I could take that lakefront walk that we were supposed to do yesterday?"

He yawned and nodded as her fingers delicately brushed back the hair out of his eyes. He captured her arm and turned, planting a soft kiss on the inside of her wrist, her skin felt so smooth under his lips.

"I'm going to go home and work for a bit, but I'll knock on the door at noon."

Luke made to sit up, but she gently pushed him back down. "Why don't you sleep a little longer? Two nights in a row sleeping in a seated position probably hasn't been nice to your body." Before he could argue, she leaned down and planted a soft kiss on his lips. "Thank you for letting me stay the night. I'll see you in a few hours." With a smile, she left.

Luke took her advice and closed his eyes, sleeping for another half hour before mustering up energy to get up and shower. The warm water eased the muscles in his back as he stood under the shower head.

Today is, hopefully, going to be a normal day.

His plan was to focus on work and look forward to his lunch date. Dressing for another hot day in shorts and a T-shirt, he made sure to put on cologne as it seemed Holly liked that. He grabbed his laptop, crashed on the couch and banged out a few hours of work.

His excitement rose as lunchtime approached. Right at noon, he heard her knock on his door. She wore jean shorts and a low-cut tank top with her hair left down just brushing her shoulders. Her purse was slung around her body, and a pair of sunglasses were already positioned over her eyes.

"Let's go, I need sunshine on my skin." She bounced

up and down, which proved to be distracting for Luke. He quickly slipped on his sneakers, and they left the building. Their apartment building stood only a few blocks away from Lake Michigan. The location was partly the reason he and Tommy had settled on their new home.

Walking hand in hand with Holly, taking in the beauty of their neighborhood, made Luke happy. Holly showed him her favorite places, pointing out how there were multi-million-dollar townhomes nestled between large '80s-styled apartment buildings. She could talk about a certain subject and just go on about it, filling the space with her thoughts and ideas, one always more random yet still entertaining than the next. One moment she was passionately speaking and the next she would stop and her eyes would light up if someone walked by with a dog.

They took the sidewalk through the park and finally onto the lakefront trail. There were large, concrete steps where people in masks were lounging about, that led down to a sidewalk where the waves were splashing up. They made their way down to the lowest level and slowed their pace, taking in the water and the skyline while keeping their distance from others.

"I've learned about you, but not your family," Luke said. "Do you have any brothers or sisters?"

"I've got two older brothers and a mom and a dad." She turned, giving him a crooked smile. "Don't I seem like the youngest child? My parents live in the suburbs where we grew up. One brother, Peter, lives in Milwaukee, and the other one, Michael, went back to school to get a master's degree and is currently in Boston. I miss them. I feel like the older we get, the better we get along, but also the farther we move away from each other." She smiled. "I think you would get along with them. Probably Michael more than Peter, the two of you would bond over nerdy computer stuff."

He feigned offense. "I'm glad you think what I do for a living, my one true passion in life, is nerdy."

Holly giggled. "Is it actually your 'one true passion'?"

Luke shook his head. "Not really. I mean I like web design; I am good at it and I'm happy doing it, but I don't know. I guess I really just wanted a job I could do from anywhere so I could travel, but I haven't gotten around to it yet." He stared into the distance at the skyline, the Hancock Tower jutting high above the rest of the buildings around it. His eyes wandered east, looking at the outline of the Ferris wheel at Navy Pier.

Her voice brought him back to the conversation. "I understand that." He studied her face as she looked out over the water. She looked peaceful with the lake air blowing her curls back, the sun shining over her freckles, her blue eyes twinkling. "I take it the theater is your uh…passion?"

She looked back to him, her eyes light with amusement. "When you've got two older brothers, you need to find some way to stand out. I figured theater was the best way to get attention." A wry grin spread over her lips. "I did all the plays and musicals in high school and college, but then realized I love performing, just not as a career. It's too difficult, full of rejection, always someone prettier, more talented than you. I realized that I could run things, be behind the scenes, and it turns out I'm good at it and it makes me happy."

Luke smiled. She was a bit of a mystery with the

way she was open and expressive about a variety of topics, but when asked a few personal questions, she tried to downplay her answers, like her life was nothing special.

She abruptly stopped walking and placed her hand on his arm. "Wait, tell me about your family. I've been talking way too much. I hate feeling like I'm giving a monologue."

Luke shook his head with a chuckle. "I also have a mom and a dad. No siblings though which I'm sure is why I've been happy living on my own for so long. But also, I've got Tommy in my life, so I have no room for any real siblings. My parents live out in Minnesota, still there, I see them probably two or three times a year, but I usually talk to them once a week. We are close, I guess. I know they miss me, want me to come back, but I like it here. They're…I don't know, they're cool? Sorry, we're just a boring normal family."

"You're not boring," she protested. "At least I don't think so, and trust me, I don't hang around boring people." She threw her arm around him and squeezed, making him chuckle.

His phone alarm signaled his lunch hour was almost over and they started making their way back home. He found himself walking slowly, trying to extend his time outside with her. He held her hand, interlacing their fingers and felt light and happy, a feeling that was sometimes foreign over the last couple of months.

Before they rounded the corner taking them to their front door, he saw someone sitting on the stoop outside the neighboring building. Luke came to a halt, it was the girl from the apartment across the alley, the roommate of the missing Jennifer Lawler. He tugged on Holly's hand

and nodded in her direction.

"We should go talk to her," she whispered, her eyes never leaving the woman.

"What would we say?" He didn't want to bother her, and she didn't look like she wanted to be bothered. Holly walked toward the girl without another word leaving him to follow.

The girl wore a light pink tank top and jeans or rather, they were wearing her. She looked gaunt with dark circles under her eyes. Her long brown hair fell over her shoulders, almost hiding her face as her attention was directed to her cell phone. Holly slowed down as she approached and, stopping a good distance away, said in a softer tone, "Hi, I'm your neighbor Holly and this is Luke."

The girl tilted her head up, with a guarded look on her face. "Um hi, I'm Lisa?" she answered, confused.

"I'm sorry, I didn't want to bother you, but I just wanted to offer my condolences. I saw about your roommate on the news, and I just wanted to ask if you were okay?"

Lisa's eyes immediately filled with tears. "How do you think I'm doing? My best friend is missing, I'm alone, and it's all my fault." She dropped her head into her hands. Holly and Luke exchanged a look. He knelt so he was eye level with the grieving girl. "What do you mean it's your fault?"

Lisa looked up, her eyes wet and full of anger. "Why are you asking me?"

"Because we know one of the other missing girls," she smoothly lied. "And we miss her, and we want to know if there is any connection."

Lisa looked back and forth between the two,

deciding they were trustworthy enough to talk to. "I went out that night, over to a friend's house. I must have left the door unlocked and she was in there, alone. I didn't help, I didn't…I left her there, open for whomever…" Her voice caught and she started to cry, full on. Luke stood back up, letting Holly comfort Lisa, and took a few steps away.

Even if Lisa had locked the door when she left, it would not have mattered. Phil, who he suspected of being the one who broke into Holly's apartment, could pick locks. He bet that Phil was probably watching them for months and waited until they were separated one night. Jennifer never stood a chance with a stalker living next to her.

Once Lisa was able to calm down, she went inside leaving them standing outside her building. Holly's jaw was clenched, nostrils flared, clearly angry. She was staring at the door Lisa had just walked through and, while Luke felt the same way, he didn't want to be caught standing here in case Phil should come out.

He put a hand on her back to start moving her toward their apartments. "Hey, let's head back."

"Good idea," she said, "go grab your things and I'll meet you on the porch in five minutes." Before he could question her choice of work venue, he stumbled over his untied shoelace. He looked up but Holly was already speeding around the corner of the building toward the door. Bending down to re-tie his shoelaces, another set of shoes came into his line of vision.

Steel toed, brown work boots stood in front of him. He lifted his gaze slowly taking in the loose-fitting jeans, blue cotton T-shirt, and the light flannel shirt layered on top of it, open, flapping in the breeze. He stood up, pleased to see he had a few inches on Phil. Up close he took in the pale complexion and bad skin. His light facial hair covered pink acne scars and thin lips and his eyes had an intensity to them made even more unsettling by the smile that didn't quite reach them.

"You're Holly's boyfriend, aren't you?" His voice was a bit higher and softer than Luke imagined.

Without missing a beat, Luke responded in a lower voice. "Yes I am. I'm sorry, she's never mentioned you, but I've seen you before, through the window."

His smile faltered a bit. "Yeah. I'm Phil. I saw you at the dumpster the other day."

Luke's insides tightened; he did not like where this exchange was going. He slowly began to step around him, heading back to the building. "Yeah, I remember. Good to see you, I've got to head back."

"I'm sure you do. I'll see you up there." Luke turned around to look at Phil, smiling with an eyebrow raised. "Because I can see you on your porch."

Luke nodded in understanding before Phil continued. "It's just crazy how we can see each other so much. It's funny, I've watched Holly on her porch for a long time, I play piano for her, but I've only just recently seen you."

Luke began to walk back toward him until he was close enough to make Phil have to tilt his head up to look at him. "Yeah, I just happened to move next to her. I may be a new sight, but you should get used to it because it'll be one you see for a long time." He stared at him, unblinking, wanting the message to sink in all the while Phil kept smiling.

He finally broke eye contact and looked past him. "Well I'm glad you've found an apartment you like so much." He looked back and said, "Good weather today, maybe I'll take a walk by the lake. Have a good day."

It wasn't until Phil was completely inside and out of view that Luke turned to see what he had been looking at. The edge of his and Holly's shared porch was jutting out into the alley, and he could see her tanned, bare legs walking around. Realizing his fists were clenched, he shook out his hands and took a deep breath. Why did he get the feeling something bad was about to happen?

Chapter Thirteen

Holly sat on the back porch, both feet on the railing, laptop against her thighs, and her eyes glued to Phil's window.

Luke came out and took his usual seat across from her. His expression was hard; his voice was full of concern. "Holly, what is going on? I thought maybe we were done sitting out here for the time being?"

She tore her gaze away from the window. His green eyes were filled with a mixture of confusion and worry, his brown curls covering his drawn brow. Holly knew this was not the time, but she could not help think how cute he looked. And the idea that he worried about her and her well being made her heart swell. She let herself sit in that warm feeling then pushed it down. She needed to focus.

"He is a monster. We know it but we just can't prove it. We are going to wait until he leaves, go in, and get proof." Her voice was low and full of anger.

Luke's eyes went wide with disbelief. "Are you insane?" At her sign to be quiet, he lowered his voice to an angry whisper. "You want to break into a possible murderer's apartment and steal something? No. Absolutely not."

She leaned back in her seat, resuming her relaxed position. "You don't have to do anything. You can be the lookout while I do it." He started to protest but she continued on in her even tone. "You have a vantage point from here. You'll be able to see if someone leaves or enters the building. We already know he keeps things in boxes in that room. While I'm checking things out in there, you can keep an eye on me."

Luke stood suddenly and began to pace around the small confines of the porch. "This is nuts. We are not doing this. You are not doing this. I'm going inside. Without a lookout you won't go."

Holly jumped up, a note of pleading in her voice. "Please, I need someone to help me. You said you'd watch my back." She crossed to him and placed her hands on his chest. "Luke. Please. I need you to do this with me. I need your help." Emotion swelled in her chest.

She didn't realize until she said it out loud, she was really starting to fall for him. It wasn't that she just needed him, she wanted him there, with her, helping her, being with her. Her hands fell to her sides, and she slowly moved back to her seat.

He stood there for a moment not moving. It took all her willpower not to turn her head and watch him debate himself. Finally, as she felt the wood boards creak, she heard Luke take his seat. Her heart lifted. Out of the corner of her eye she saw his hand inch across the table, but at the last second, he pulled back.

"Thank you," she said quietly, without moving her focus from the window in the building across the way. "He's still in there, but in the other room at the moment. Once he leaves, I'll climb the fire escape outside his open window."

For the next hour, neither of them spoke. Holly still felt Luke's anger and annoyance at her, yet he stayed with her. Phil continued walking in and out of his room, doing various tasks. Finally, he sat on the bed appearing to ready himself to leave.

Her spine straightened. "This is it."

Luke looked up, swallowing hard. "I still don't want you to do this."

She looked over at him, his green eyes making a silent plea. "I know, but we need to do something."

Reaching across the table, he grabbed both of her hands, forcing her to turn her whole body in his direction, and stared at her straight on. "If he comes back, I won't be there to protect you. So, if I can't stop you from going over there, can you at least promise me you'll stay mainly in the bedroom where I can see you? Please?"

Even with the adrenaline building, Holly began to feel scared. With all the things they've seen, he always remained calm and collected but now, seeing real fear in his eyes made her uncomfortable. She needed to go before she chickened out.

"I'll get over there, do a quick sweep of the other rooms, and then stay in the bedroom."

She looked over at the window as Phil walked out the bedroom door. Both she and Luke stood and looked over the ledge to their right where they had a decent view of the corner of the building's entrance. A moment later Phil walked out and turned right, heading down the street.

Their wooden porch was directly across from the back stairs of the neighboring building. While the buildings themselves were a good distance apart, the fire escapes had clearly been an afterthought and hastily added to the buildings. They each jutted out over the alleyway, practically touching each other. In Holly's opinion, it was probably a fire hazard, but she had never been more thankful for that than right now.

She began to hoist herself up and onto the porch railing; suddenly Luke's hands were on her waist, giving her a boost. Standing up and holding onto the beam with her left hand, she reached out with her right hand and grabbed onto the fire escape of the building next door. Now, reaching across the space, she felt like it was a million miles away when it couldn't have been more than a few feet.

She hesitated but heard Luke behind her. "I got you, I won't let you fall."

Emboldened she reached out and grabbed the railing with her other hand and, taking a deep breath, her right foot followed then finally her left foot. In one quick motion, she swung her body over the railing and looked back in disbelief.

Luke stared at her, a relieved smile on his face. "Hurry up."

With a nod, she ducked in through Phil's bedroom window.

The room was a decent size but felt bigger due to lack of personal things in the space. There was a queen-sized bed in the middle of the room with a lightweight plaid comforter on top. Next to it was a bedside table with an electric alarm clock but nothing else. Against the wall with the window was a trunk and small upright piano. On the wall opposite the bed was a dresser with a small television. A wall mirror hung next to it. She looked back over her shoulder to see Luke staring at her, hands gripping the rail. He gave her a quick nod and she mirrored it, walking out into the rest of the apartment.

She would describe it the same as she would his bedroom: boring. Nothing personal hung on the walls, no framed photos on side tables or shelves. Nothing. She went into the kitchen and opened the fridge which to her relief was filled with takeout containers, but no human heads.

Okay. I can rule out a Jeffrey Dahmer copycat.

She looked in the hall closet to find three coats and two pairs of boots. She looked in the entertainment stand drawers and found random cords. Giving a quick look at his bookshelf, she saw it was filled with encyclopedias and informational books, making him seem extra creepy in her opinion. She would have expected sci-fi or fantasy books or maybe some biographies. Satisfied, or rather unsatisfied that there was no incriminating evidence, she went back to the bedroom. Looking out the window again, she saw Luke in the same stance but slightly more relaxed now that she was back in view.

Deciding to start with the closet, she turned her attention there. Flinging the door open she saw shirts and pants hanging, on the bottom were a few cardboard boxes. She pulled out the first box and opened it, full of books, the one that they had seen the cops pull out. Quickly closing it, she went to the next one which was full of old, slightly dusty children's toys. She suspected they were his from childhood. The last box was full of old clothes.

This she sifted through carefully, making sure none of them were the torn shirt stolen from her house. Nothing. She looked over the rest of the closet and, deciding it was evidence free, moved on. She looked everywhere, under the bed, in the dresser drawers, the nightstand. Each time she came up with nothing.

Looking out the window at Luke, he glanced to his right and back at her shaking his head meaning she still had more time. She moved to the trunk, the last possible place, and opened it slowly. This was where Phil hid his mess. It was full of random papers, photos, and more books. Holly started to sift through it. She read some of the papers; bills and invoices, looking closely she saw they were for the storage locker he held, going back to a year ago. She dug further and heard a crinkling of what sounded like a plastic bag, she paused, wasn't the torn shirt in the plastic bag?

"Holly."

She bolted up to the window, Luke's eyes were wide. "He's home. Get out. Now."

She bent back down to the trunk, she had only a moment to dig out the bag. Her finger felt the plastic and she pulled, sending papers scattering on the floor. She fell to her knees and swept everything into her arms and threw it all into the trunk. Slamming down the lid, bag in hand, she ducked through the window and went out onto the fire escape.

"Catch this." she threw the bag across the space, and he caught it, throwing it on the seat behind him without taking his eyes off her.

"Get your ass over here, now."

She swung herself onto the other side of the railing as she heard the sound of a door closing, Phil had entered his apartment. Panic overtook as she locked eyes with Luke. He reached his long body over the edge and grabbed Holly's outstretched arms. She barely needed to jump across as he lifted her up and over the railing like she weighed nothing.

As soon as she was safely over the railing, she grabbed the bag on the chair, ran and opened her apartment door and threw it inside. She immediately looked over at the window. Phil walked into his bedroom looking at his phone, seemingly unaware she'd been in there just moments ago.

Letting out the breath she'd not realized she'd been holding, she turned toward Luke. "We did it…"

The celebration died on her lips as he abruptly turned and left the porch.

She sat back down. He left his laptop out on the table, so he had to come back at some point. She looked up through his screen door, and saw Luke pacing in and out of view, hands rubbing his temples. Guilt overtook her, she did not want to be the cause of a temple rub.

Oh God, I've made him complicit in breaking and entering. He must be freaking out. Is it bad that I'm not freaking out?

Wanting to apologize, she cautiously made her way to the screen door and slowly pushed it open. "Luke?" she called in a soft voice, "I'm so sor—".

Her apology was cut short as Luke, in one swift motion turned, pulled her in, and pressed her up against the wall, fiercely kissing her. His lips crushed against hers, moving fast. His hands were on each side of her face pulling hard as his body pushed hers against the wall. His tongue darted fast in and out of her mouth.

Holly couldn't think, she couldn't breathe, her toes curled. She grabbed his shoulders and held on trying, if possible, to get her body even closer to his. She wanted more and opened her mouth wider, inviting him in farther, nipping his bottom lip with her teeth. Her hands moved down, going beneath the hem of his shirt and started their ascent, this time underneath the thin fabric. She wanted to get her hands on him for so long and now she felt like she was unwrapping a present. She could feel the muscles tense as she ran her fingers over his abs. Her hands changed direction again and headed south for his waistband. His arousal pushed against her lower abdomen. As soon as her fingers reached the elastic band of his basketball shorts, he abruptly pulled back. As fast as he had pushed her against the wall, he was across the room, breathing heavily.

Trying to catch her breath, she was lightheaded and suddenly cold now that his body was off hers. Luke placed his hands on either side above her and bent his head toward her, foreheads pressing against each other. His eyes closed as he struggled to even his breath.

"Please," he whispered, "don't do something like that again."

The pleading tone in his voice was such a contrast from the passion of the kiss. Overcome by his concern, she was taken over by the impulse to comfort him, comfort him for something she did. She lifted her hands to his face and cupped it, her thumb gently stroking the stubble along his cheek.

"I'm sorry. I won't," she whispered. He opened his eyes, their faces mere inches apart. "We okay?"

He nodded and slowly un-bent himself, mumbled something about using the bathroom and walked away.

Holly couldn't help but smile, just now catching her breath. She peeled herself off the wall and slowly made her way out to the porch. Obviously, she thought to herself, she would not do anything crazy, but if scaring him warranted that kind of response she might want to do it more often. Holly had never been kissed like that, and even if she had, it could not have compared to Luke. The power of his body against her, the self-control he had…it made her want him even more. She eased down into her chair and turned her attention to her forgotten computer checking on all the emails she had missed in the last hour. Luke came out through the door and sat giving Holly a look that sent vibrations through her body.

"All good?" she asked, planting a smirk on her face.

"Not quite, but I will be."

Before she could come up with a witty retort, a yell burst their bubble of sexual tension. Their heads turned, following the outburst coming from across the alleyway.

As Phil roared, items flew past the window, landing on various pieces of furniture in his apartment. As Holly realized the items all came from the area where the trunk rested, panic started bubbling in her chest.

"That's the area where I found the bag," she whispered.

Luke's eyes went wide. "Okay, slowly get up and stretch and say you need a drink then grab the laptop and go inside. Just act normal in case he looks up."

She nodded and did exactly what he said. As she stretched her hands high over her head, she turned her back to the window and whispered, "Why did I have to stretch?"

He gave her a mischievous smile and gestured at her body. "So I could get this view."

She looked down and saw that he was looking at her breasts which were now pushed together and lifted. She immediately dropped her arms and put her hands on her hips. "Now is not the time."

Suppressing his grin, he nodded. She continued following his instructions and made it to her door. She turned her head back to say something when her eyes locked on the window.

Phil stood there, staring at her, eyes wide, lips in a

thin line of fury. Attempting to play it cool, she continued into the house. The moment she was out of sight of the window; the fear that was held at bay overtook her, and her knees buckled, sending her stumbling, grabbing the kitchen counter for support. She looked back out through her screen door to see Luke looking at her, clearly wanting to help her. She steadied herself and reached up with trembling hands, grabbing a glass and filling it up under the faucet. She looked back outside to see Luke gather his things and casually walk into his house.

She shakily made her way to the front of her apartment and opened the door to see Luke barging out of his and straight toward her. The moment he was close enough, he gathered her up in his arms and held her tight. This was her happy place now, in his arms with his scent around her, she felt safe, she felt possibly…loved?

He practically carried her to the couch and sat them both down. "I've been thinking…" He stopped and then started again. "I know we haven't known each other too long…" He stopped again.

Emotionally exhausted, Holly said, "Just spit it out."

He looked down at his hands. "I have a family friend who has a cabin up in Wisconsin. It's only two hours away. I want to go up there, and I would like you to come with. It would just be a few days."

He got up and grabbed the plastic bag containing the shirt. "We call Officers Shane and Martinez, turn this in, rent a car, and just go for a few days. We get out of the way while justice is uh, served or something. What do you think?"

Holly rose. "When can we leave?"

Luke smiled, relief flooded his face. "Let's call the

officers tonight and leave first thing in the morning? I'll set everything up."

She nodded and went into her room to start packing. The sooner she could get away from here, the better.

Chapter Fourteen

Officer Martinez raised an eyebrow at Holly, his expression full of doubt. "Tell me one more time how you got the shirt back."

She felt heat rising up into her cheeks from her neck, but she stood her ground. "It was balled up behind the dumpster. I'm sure he didn't think we'd look for it there again."

By his face and body language, she knew the cop wasn't buying her answer. "Interesting. I didn't see it when I checked outside for those paper towels."

Offering a smirk, his partner, Officer Shane, continued to take notes on a pad. "Guess you just missed it, but this is good. Now we might have physical evidence."

Officer Martinez said, "We have to test the blood on this shirt, see if it matches any of the girls. We also will check for his DNA, otherwise we can't tie it to him. It'll take a while—backlog at the lab, but we'll let you know as soon as possible."

Luke slid a protective arm around Holly's shoulders. "We're going to leave the city for a few days. The well...attention from him has gotten a lot more aggressive, and it's really uncomfortable."

Officer Shane looked up sharply. "Aggressive?"

Feeling silly, looking down at her feet, she mumbled, "It's really—he's just—it's kind of scary."

Martinez changed his tone. "In that case, you guys are doing the right thing. Get out of here for a few days until things calm down. We performed another check up on him, but nothing seemed out of the ordinary."

Officer Shane put his notepad back in his pocket and slapped Martinez on the back. "We've got everything we need. We'll be in touch."

Grabbing the bag containing the shirt, they both left, Martinez putting a comforting hand on Holly's shoulder before closing the door behind them.

She turned to Luke who was scowling at the closed door. "At least they think we're being safe about this... so I guess I'll see you tomorrow morning?"

Luke replaced the scowl on his face with an uncomfortable expression. "I think you should stay over at my place again. I don't like the idea of you being alone." Seeing the longing look she sent toward her bedroom door, he continued, "Or how about I come sleep on the couch?"

Holly smiled. "I couldn't do that to you again, you need to sleep in a normal bed."

"No," he protested. "I'm totally fine to do it."

She shook her head. "We're being silly. Why don't you just sleep in my bed with me?" When he hesitated, she said, "Or, you can take Kate's bed if you don't think you'll be comfortable..."

"No," he interrupted. "I'll share your bed with you."

Luke left and was back within ten minutes having packed his bag for the next two days and changed into sleepwear. As it was still early, the two of them decided to snuggle up on the couch and watch TV.

When it came time for bed, Holly felt awkward. Typically if she invited a man to sleep over, sleeping was the last thing they did, usually having other activities to occupy them. With Luke, it was the only thing on the menu tonight. She knew they had to leave early the next day, so they actually had to get a good night's rest. Having changed into an oversized T-shirt and sleep shorts, she switched off the light and slid under the covers next to Luke, very aware of his large, shirtless frame lying next to hers.

Yeah, I'm not going to fall asleep easily tonight.

Attempting to make it easier on her, she turned her back to him saying a quick "Good night" and shut her eyes tight, willing sleep to come. Luke shifted, the mattress creaking at the movement. A moment later his arm snaked across her waist and his hand rested on her abdomen, dangerously close to cupping her breast.

"Good night, Holly," he whispered with what she swore was a hint of a smile in his voice.

His warm breath sent shivers down her spine; she knew what he was trying to do. She felt the heat of his arm, his hand, and an excitement grew in her belly. She scooted back farther into his embrace, her backside wiggling against his groin. He let out a slow breath and she smiled; they could both play this game.

Clearing his throat, he resituated himself, letting his hand travel north, and his thumb landed right over her nipple. She tried to control her breathing but found it difficult with the heat of his hand on her chest. Lying in the dark next to each other, not talking, not kissing, just touching was incredibly erotic. Her hand covered his, and she absentmindedly stroked his knuckles with her thumb as she pushed her bottom a bit more into him and was delighted when she felt him grow against her. His hand moved down to her belly and pulled her back, harder into his groin so she could feel his arousal as he began to slowly move back and forth.

Holly felt the tip of his shaft poking her from behind. Her shorts had ridden up, and he positioned himself so as he moved, he pushed against her. Holly gasped and grabbed onto the pillow holding her head and closed her eyes. Luke continued his slow torture until Holly was so worked up she actually moaned, causing him to stop.

Her eyes flew open, and she felt the bed move as Luke chuckled. She turned around and saw Luke turning his back to her. "Jeez, I'm tired. Well long day tomorrow, goodnight, Hol."

She could not believe he just left her there, unsatisfied. He thought it was funny? She turned back to her original position with a huff, she would get him back tomorrow.

****

The next morning Luke gave Holly's arm a gentle shake. "Hey. I've got to go pick up the car but I didn't want you to wake up and be alone." He gave her a small smile while rubbing his eyes, still trying to wake up.

She smiled sleepily. "Let me get up with you and I'll go get ready." She grabbed his arm and attempted to move herself up into a sitting position and ended up falling into his lap earning an 'Oomph' from him as her forearms crashed into his groin.

"Oh God, I'm sorry." He grimaced, clearly trying to smile through the pain, and grabbed her arms with his strong hands, righting her.

Despite taking his time to stand up, he chuckled. "That is one way to wake up in the morning."

"At least it's an interesting start to the trip?"

Luke rented the car and after picking up Holly, they

hit the road. The car snaked through the narrow streets of Lakeview onto the main roads, taking them past closed bars and stores. After getting onto the main highway, they played road trip games, listened to music, chatted about everything and nothing for the next two hours.

Well, almost everything, they did tend to steer clear of the topic of Phil which in Luke's opinion was completely fine. He just wanted time with Holly when she didn't feel scared that someone was watching them. Hopefully by physically removing themselves from the situation, in a place where he was sure he could protect the both of them, they could act like themselves and just enjoy each other's company. He thought he really felt something with Holly. She seemed to drive him crazy. Crazy with fear, crazy with concern, with lust, she pushed all his buttons.

Someone who did that to him, made him feel this way, was someone he did not want to lose.

Finally, after two separate bathroom breaks, they pulled onto a street lined with trees and bushes, every so often there was a mailbox and entrance of a driveway peeking out of the wilderness. Luke drove all the way down the street and pulled into the last driveway on the right before a line of trees created a dead end. He drove slowly down the gravel path that led to an opening where a cute brown cottage-style house stood. Holly peered through the car window. "This is so cute. Who does it belong to again?"

He parked easily as he answered. "It's the house of a family friend. They are currently in Minnesota, so they haven't been here for a while. I come up here every now and then to check on it for them. Let me show you the best part." He came around the car and grabbed Holly's hand and led her around the house, toward the backyard. As soon as the lake came into view, Holly gasped.

Off the back of the house was a three-season room which connected to a large wooden porch, in the middle of which stood a stone firepit. A state-of-the-art grill stood off to the side, and cushy patio furniture was scattered over the rest of the space. A covered hot tub stood off to the side. The backyard of the cabin was covered in lush green grass which sloped down to a large wooden dock and out onto the lake where a small motorboat was docked. A two seated rocking chair sat on the dock, perfect for watching the sunset on. Luke looked over at Holly who was taking it all in, awe on her face. This was just the reaction he wanted and felt joy at being able to give it to her.

"This is perfect. I can't wait to see the rest of the house."

After grabbing the bags, he led her inside. It was an updated four-bedroom house. The décor was what you would expect for a cabin, lots of wood accents, dark greens and blues and browns, very woodsy. It was a large open plan with the den being the center of the house with a large brown leather couch covered in blankets and pillows. A large television stood against one wall with floor to ceiling wooden bookshelves on either side. Taking a step up, they entered the kitchen which was completely updated with marble countertops, new appliances, and dark wooden cabinets. Large bay windows covered the back wall of the kitchen with a cozy nook and breakfast table nestled below it.

The tour continued upstairs where he led her to the bedrooms. The first three bedrooms were more or less the same with a queen-sized bed in the middle of the room, a dresser, closet, and nightstand. The fourth room was the master bedroom. The floor was covered in a fluffy rug sitting on top of which was a large, king-sized bed with a big wooden frame. Right off the room was the master bathroom which featured a Jacuzzi tub and a rain shower.

Luke smiled when Holly's eyes went wide. "You can take this room; I'll grab the one down the hall."

He'd slept here so many times he didn't really care which room he ended up in at night. What he really wanted was to end up in Holly's bed, but this was a time to relax, not to make assumptions that she wanted the same thing as him at least not until she gave him a clear "go" sign.

She looked as if she wanted to say something and then thought better of it and continued to look around. After a moment of slightly awkward silence, he cleared his throat. "Do you want to stay here and freshen up while I run into town and grab food? We can cook out on the grill tonight."

Holly looked relieved. "I could use a quick nap in an actual bed. Are you sure you can go alone?"

Luke nodded, he turned to leave then stopped, and turned back to Holly. He closed the space between them and lowered his head to give her a small kiss on the cheek. "I'll be back soon."

Her arms snaked up and around his shoulders, keeping him against her in a hug. "Thank you so much from bringing me here."

He felt emotion well up in his chest as he embraced her and smiled, his face hidden in her hair. After a moment he let go and straightened up slowly. Looking into her eyes, Luke felt that familiar spark between them.

I could stay, he thought, *and turn that spark into a fire, I mean the bed is right there.*

He forced himself to walk out of the room, promising himself he would explore that later in a more romantic way.

Luke drove to the downtown area of the small Wisconsin town and went to the grocery store. It felt like a long time since he got the chance to grill out. He bought two steaks, a variety of vegetables and potatoes for tonight and burgers and hot dogs for the next day in addition to cereal for breakfast. He bought beers and wine figuring it was a vacation, they should unwind. He wanted to cook her a meal tonight that she would not forget, something to knock her off her feet.

When he arrived back at the cabin he entered as quietly as possible, only to be greeted with the sound of laughter. Confused, he walked around the stairs to the couch area to see Holly wrapped in a blanket, watching a movie.

"Oh, you're back." She started to get up, but he gestured her to keep her seat.

"Let me put this away and I'll come join you or we can go out on the lake?" Holly perked up at the last suggestion, a look of excitement on her face.

"Lake please. I'll go change into a bathing suit." She scrambled up and out of sight as Luke walked into the kitchen and hurriedly put everything away.

Running quickly upstairs, Luke threw on some swim trunks and a T-shirt. Coming out of his room, he stopped in his tracks. Holly came out of her room at the same time and was holding her tank-top and a towel in one hand. She wore a navy-blue bikini top and jean shorts and looked…well good enough to stop him in his tracks. Her curvaceous body and sun kissed skin looked so soft that he resisted the urge to reach out and run his hand up and down her side. Her hair was up in a messy bun, and a sly smile was on her face.

"You just gonna stand there and look at me or you gonna drive me around on a boat?" He laughed and they both ran out of the house, only stopping to grab a few beers first.

The boat was on the smaller side, big enough for about six people. Holly and Luke were able to spread out, sitting on opposite ends of the boat. Holly laid out on the cushioned seats on the front end of the boat. As he slowly backed them out of the dock, she shimmied out of her jeans shorts and stretched, letting the sun warm every inch of her skin.

Driving them around the lake at a slow pace, listening to the radio, drinking a beer, and every now and then watching Holly, he decided this was the life. Barely anyone else was on the lake that day and after a while, Luke dropped anchor. By now the sun was high in the sky and he was sweating through his shirt. He pulled it off and looked over at Holly whose eyes were closed, and toes were tapping along with the song that was playing.

Slowly, he eased into the warm water and swam around to the front end of the boat. Making sure that Holly did not hear him scoop a handful of water, he whipped it onto the boat and heard a yelp. Holly, glistening with water, looked over the side of the boat, a look of disbelief on her face.

"Oh, you did not just do that."

He smiled, floating back a little bit. "What are you

going to do about it?"

Holly disappeared and after a beat launched herself over the side of the boat, her body curled into a ball. The splash hit Luke in the face full on. He continued to splutter and wipe his eyes when Holly's head popped back up from the water, laughing.

Narrowing his eyes, he treaded water. "Oh, you are so dead."

Holly shrieked as he lunged toward her. She dove under water and popped up a few feet away causing him to raise an amused eyebrow.

"I never told you that I swam in high school, did I?" he said, lowering himself predatorily into the water so only his eyes became visible. Holly's smile faltered as she turned and tried to swim farther out but was no match for Luke. His long arms and legs propelled him to her in seconds, and he grabbed her around the waist. She turned in his grasp so they were face to face.

"Well, you're just full of surprises." Holly wrapped her legs around Luke's waist as he continued to tread water. Her arms snaked around his neck, and she pulled him to her lips. The water lapped up his chin as her tongue opened his lips. Without thinking, Luke put his hands on her waist. The two of them began to sink, and he quickly put his arms back up to help tread, keeping them both afloat.

Holly giggled, a sound that made his stomach do a flip with excitement. "Guess you can't touch me unless you want us to go under."

She extracted herself and swam around him, re-hooking her ankles so she was now on his back. Her mouth found his earlobe and sent shivers up and down his spine. Her warm breath lapped against his neck, and her teeth grazed his skin. It was getting harder to continue to tread, his waning concentration and growing arousal making the task more difficult.

"You keep that up and you're going to have to be the one to keep us afloat."

He was met with a deep throaty laugh as she switched to the other side of his head. "I think you're doing a pretty good job of it." Her tongue traced the underside of his earlobe and down his neck.

His swim trunks were now uncomfortably tight, he couldn't take it anymore. "Hold your breath," he growled and unhooked her legs from his body.

Luke quickly turned, facing Holly. His hand pulled her head to him, crushing her lips to his, and they both went under the water, mouths still connected. They sank together, neither one letting go until they ran out of air. Their bodies unlocked and they both bobbed up to the surface, gasping for air. Their eyes locked and they stayed like that, silent only for the sound of water rippling around them. Suddenly she blinked, and uncertainty flashed in her eyes. A moment later, she splashed water at him, bringing the lightheartedness back.

Luke swam back to the boat, grabbing two noodles, and the couple floated, talked, laughed, and listened to music for the next hour. He found himself wondering what that moment was. Did he take things too far, make Holly nervous? She flipped the switch fast, and he wanted her to be comfortable and just follow her lead. When their fingers pruned, they hopped back onto the boat. Luke drove a few more laps around the lake and headed back to the house.

"I think I'm going to lie out in the sun for a bit if you

want to join."

Luke shook his head. "That's okay, you go relax, tan, whatever. I'm gonna go inside and check my email then start prepping the food for dinner."

Holly smiled lazily and laid her towel in the grass, placing herself on top of it face down. He watched her settle down, lingering for a moment on her perfectly rounded backside, and then headed up to the house to prepare for the night ahead.

Chapter Fifteen

Holly stepped out of the rain shower, drying off with a fluffy white towel. The water pressure here was amazing, and the temperature became hot instantly. It was something she couldn't always count on in her apartment.

If she was being honest with herself, the whole day had been amazing. Relaxing in the sun, going on a boat, and just being out of the city in general put her in a better mood. She hadn't thought about Phil once in the last twelve hours, and it was all thanks to Luke.

There was another thing that made today... memorable.

She had seen Luke shirtless before but being with him, in the water, and then afterwards with that underwater kiss... She could feel herself falling for him, hard, and it scared her in that moment. She was happy he hadn't questioned or pushed anything and was thankful he went inside afterward, leaving her out in the sun by herself for the rest of the afternoon.

She walked into her room and looked down at her suitcase. When she packed for this getaway, she wasn't scared of feelings and went for a "casual and sexy" style with her wardrobe. She brought shorts, low cut flowy shirts, and all of her laciest, dirtiest lingerie.

Just because you brought it doesn't mean you have to use it.

She finally chose a matching set of lacy, black underwear and wore a thin black T-shirt and jean shorts over it. After lying out today she developed more color on her face so she went light on the makeup, only putting on mascara and a little bit of product in her hair. She took a deep breath, reminding herself one more time that nothing had to happen, and went downstairs.

Looking through the window she saw Luke on the patio, working the grill. Everything she had just assured herself of flew out of her mind at the sight of him. His tight gray T-shirt pulled as his arms moved, using the towel thrown over his shoulder to wipe his hands clean. Her eyes lowered to his khaki covered bottom, appreciating the view. Now she was glad she wore sexy underwear.

Walking to the kitchen, she poured herself a large glass of wine, hoping the cold alcohol would calm her.

It's okay to change your mind again—she thought—*just have fun.*

She walked out the back door and asked, "Can I help with anything?"

Luke turned around smiling, his green eyes lighting up, making Holly's breath hitch. "Everything is currently cooking, but I wouldn't say no to a beer?"

Holly saluted and turned back into the kitchen where she immediately slapped her palm on her face.

Why the hell can't I just act normal?

Grabbing the beer and the bottle of wine she went back out and sat at the table, kicking her feet up on the chair next to her. "So chef, what are you making for me?"

"Steak, potatoes, and grilled veggie kabobs." He went and opened the grill, letting the smell waft over, causing her mouth to water. A man who knew his way around a kitchen was such a turn on and she, once again, was thankful she packed with a certain mood in mind.

"If it's anything like any of the other meals you've made me, it's going to be amazing." Luke lowered his head, back to the food looking bashful, making Holly's tummy fill with butterflies.

"So how did you become a top chef? Born with the gift?"

He gave a loud 'ha' and took a quick swig of beer. "Definitely not. My mom stayed at home with me until high school and then went back to work. After that, some days I would be on my own for dinner if both my parents were working late, and I just got sick of pizza or sandwiches." He started to plate the food. "Then some nights when my parents were home, I would watch them cook, learn from them. Then I started getting nerdy and watched cooking shows in my free time. I just loved it, and I loved being able to make people happy with my food." He shrugged but Holly was touched, that was exactly the way she felt about cooking. "Anyways, here it is." He set the plates on the table and sat across from her as the two began to dig in.

Holly watched him as he ate, completely at ease. "You're in your element here."

He looked up from his plate with a lopsided grin. "What are you talking about?"

She sat back in her seat. "I mean I've seen you in the city and I've seen you out here with land around you and a lake at your feet, and I got to say, you seem…happier up here, away from everything."

He mirrored her laid-back posture, beer in hand. "I wouldn't say that. I mean, I like the outdoors yes, but I also like walking down the block and getting my groceries rather than sit in a car for a ten-minute drive. I don't know...my work can be done from anywhere which is nice, but I think I like what I have right now. The ability to get away, but still have a permanent place in a city."

"You think you'll have your own cabin one day?"

"Oh definitely. Even if I were to move away, I would still buy a place like this one day. Have a reason to come back to the Midwest."

The thought of Luke moving away gave her an unexpected feeling of sadness. In her opinion, he belonged here, and she wanted to belong with him. She shook the idea out of her head, there she went again having those serious thoughts that would end up freaking her out later. Her attention turned back to her plate as she attempted to keep her tone light. "Then you'll have your own place to bring girls to, rather than your family friend's house."

"They'll only see my cabin if they wrap me up in a murder investigation like you have."

Holly's shoulders slumped as she proceeded to drain, then refill her wine. "I'm sorry about all this." She was careful to keep her eyes averted, she knew one look into his green eyes would send her emotions flowing out of her like a spilled glass. She concentrated on finishing her meal.

"You know I'm not sorry about any of it right?"

Holly snorted, continuing to look down until she felt his hand reach across the table and cup her chin, gently tilting her face up. Her eyes locked with his.

"I'm not sorry at all. Yes, it's crazy and scary, but we did the right thing. In a roundabout way, I'm glad we reported it because it led to me getting to us spending a few days alone together." His green eyes bored into her, so sincere, and made Holly's eyes start to well up.

He let go, and she quickly wiped her eyes. "Thanks for saying that."

His gaze still hadn't relented. "I wasn't saying it to make you feel better. I was saying it because it's true."

Her chest started to rise and fall at a faster pace. She grabbed her wine to take a sip and give her a moment, she didn't know how to respond.

Luke took it as a sign to continue. "Holly, I really love being around you. I love spending time with you, and I don't want to stop."

Swallowing hard, she got up grabbing the now empty plates and walked inside the house. She needed a moment to compose herself, take in what he just said. Could this be happening, could things be working out just the way she wanted? Unfortunately, her moment alone was short lived as he followed her into the kitchen.

Coming up right behind her as she placed the plates into the sink, he positioned himself to trap her between the counter and his body. She looked over her shoulder and up at him through her eyelashes.

"Tell me you don't feel the same way. I promise I didn't bring you here to make you feel uncomfortable, but in the water today and every time we've kissed before..." He took a shaky breath and ran a hand through his hair, Holly looked down at her feet. "I know you feel it too, but I won't pursue this if you don't want me to."

Her hands gripped the edge of the countertop, knuckles turning white, she could feel her heart thumping in her chest, the blood rushing in her ears. She turned on the spot and shyly looked up at him through her lashes, locking eyes with him again and whispered,

Emilie Barage

"I do want you to."

Luke grabbed her, picking her up and placing her on top of the counter, and crashed his lips to hers. He kissed her hungrily. His hands slid down underneath her knees and pulled flush against him. Holly did one better and wrapped her legs around his waist, her hands flew to his hair, tugging on his curls. Her own hunger matched his as she molded her body to his, wanting to touch every inch of him.

His hands slowly glided up her bare legs, leaving goosebumps. They traveled over her shorts and found their way under the hem of her T-shirt where they skimmed her lower back. His hands felt warm on her bare skin. As she began to tilt backward, his palm splayed across her back keeping her upright. Meanwhile his mouth moved off hers and started trailing kisses down her neck, earning a small moan of arousal from Holly's mouth. She began to squirm, but one of Luke's hands flew up and cupped her head while his other kept moving up her back finally hitting the lace.

He paused in his actions and asked in a low, husky voice, "Did you put something special on for me?"

All she could do was nod as she continued to pant. A look crossed his face which Holly could only describe as 'someone who could not wait to unwrap a present just presented to them.'

Holly smiled, untangled her hand from his hair, and slowly moved it down his body. "Did you want to see what I put on? Because I can show you here or I can show you upstairs."

On that last word her hand had reached its destination and cupped his bulging erection through his shorts. He gasped with pleasure and growled, "We're

134

going upstairs, now."

Pulling her off the counter and into his arms, he started moving quickly toward the stairs. Holly squealed in delight, grabbing onto his shoulders to keep from falling. Once he got to the stairs, she decided she didn't feel like waiting and started nibbling on his ear. He paused mid step and threw out a hand to steady himself on the banister. "You can't do that to me without a warning. "

Feeling devilish, she continued nibbling on his ear, working her way down his neck gently biting, kissing, and licking. Luke kept climbing the stairs, now at a slower pace but still with determination. He paused on the landing, panting, and Holly drew back expecting another comment, but instead he kissed her on the mouth with such ferocity it took her breath away. Feeling slightly dazed, Luke grinned then practically ran up the stairs into the master bedroom with her still in his arms.

He gently loosened his grip, standing at the foot of the bed, as she slid down his body. She took a small step back and crossed her arms grabbing the hem of her shirt, pulling it up over her head. There was a sharp intake of breath as Luke stared at her. The thin fabric covered her breasts but was so fine it was practically see-through. He closed the space between them, his hands starting on her hips and slowly moving up to cup and massage her breasts as he kissed her neck. Meanwhile Holly made use of her hands and began undoing the button and zipper to his shorts, reaching in and taking hold of what she felt earlier, no fabric separating them now. Luke let out a soft noise, his hands squeezing her in a moment of surprise, giving Holly the confidence to continue her exploration.

She began to massage him with one hand, pushing

his shorts and briefs down around his hips with the other one. He helped her, shaking the layers off and stepping out of them while simultaneously leading her backward against the bed. Holly sat on the edge of the bed, leaning back into a reclined position propped up on her elbows as Luke shed his T-shirt, giving her a view of his body in all its glory. His tanned skin covered the well-toned muscles of his arms and shoulders. He turned to throw his shirt down, and her eyes immediately went to the part of him she had first noticed upon seeing him, his butt, and he did not disappoint. Perfectly rounded and smooth, he must also have been doing squats in addition to those weights because it might have been just the best looking ass she'd ever seen. He turned back to her, his excitement in full view now.

He bent down, hands undoing her shorts' clasp. "We should get these off."

She gently brushed his hands away and got off the bed. "Why don't you sit down for a moment, you've been doing all the work here."

She pushed his chest and he sat on the edge of the bed, an amused look on his face. Holly shimmied out of her shorts and Luke's smile was wiped clean off his face, a look of desire replacing it. The bottom half of her set was a boy shorts cut, perfectly cupping her own ass cheeks. He sat there, staring, and she smirked and feigned concern, looking down. "Is this not special enough?"

He nodded his head vigorously. "Uh-huh" was all he managed to get out.

Holly smiled, feeling confident and sexy as she walked toward him and stood in between his legs giving him a kiss on the lips. He attempted to touch her, but she dodged his hands. "Not yet," she whispered. Her lips trailing kisses from his mouth down to his chest. The lower she kissed, the slower she went until she finally knelt and took him in her mouth.

"Jesus, Hol."

Holly slowly slid her mouth up and down his length, flicking her tongue underneath his shaft. She continued to do so, gradually quickening her pace, delighting in the way his hips gyrated with the movement. Luke's hands balled into fists, pressed against his forehead, eyes closed.

"If you keep doing that…" His strained voice was cut off by Holly's mouth tightening even more around him. She felt a small bead of liquid hit her tongue before suddenly in one fast motion he growled. "Enough."

He grabbed her arms, pulling her up onto the bed and flipping them so he was now on top. Then, faster still, he scooted back, one foot on the ground and one knee on the bed, sliding her panties off. Before Holly could say anything, he threw her ankles over his shoulder and bent down to start pleasuring her with his mouth.

The wet warmth of his mouth made her moan loudly. His tongue tickled and teased her, causing her to pant with desire, her hands instantly flew and tangled themselves in his curly hair, tugging, needing something to hold onto.

"Luke, please I—"

She was cut off by another involuntary moan as he added his finger into the mix. Holly started to move her hips in time with his hand. His movements became faster and faster until she was brought to climax. She grabbed a pillow strewn above her head and shoved it against her mouth, muffling her climactic shriek. Spent, her hands dropped to her sides, her breathing ragged, as she came back down to earth from the pleasure.

Luke looked up and smiled. "You know we're the only ones here, you can be as loud as you want." She threw the pillow at him, giggling. He raised his eyebrow. "I've been wanting to do that to you for a while now."

Holly smiled lazily, her hands now resting above her head. "Well, you were very good at it."

He gently put her feet down on the bed and stood. "I'm not done yet." He sped out of the room coming back a moment later with a bag in hand. Rummaging around, he finally pulled out a box of condoms. Looking extremely focused he took one and unwrapped it, slipping it on.

She scooted back on the bed, sitting up to pull the bralette over her head, and lay back down. Holly saw his muscles tighten as he looked up, his cock twitched in excitement. Gently, he climbed on top of her. His mouth found its way to her breasts, sucking and grazing her nipples with his teeth, Holly instantly felt the buildup start inside her again.

"Luke." He looked up, his eyes hooded with desire. Without breaking eye contact, he slowly moved up her body until their faces were level. As his lips touched hers, he entered her in one smooth stroke. She gasped against his mouth, and he stilled, staying like that, a look of concern flashed in his eyes as he pulled his face away from her.

"Did I hurt you? We can stop right now if you want." His arms held him above her, shaking slightly.

Holly vehemently shook her head. "No, no I'm okay it's just…been a while." She brought her hands up and gently cupped the sides of his face and smiled. "I'm okay, I promise."

The worry was wiped from his face as he slowly started to move again, in and out. After a few strokes, and Holly encouraging him with her moans and movements, he began to thrust harder. He buried his face against her neck and hair while her nails dug into his shoulder blades.

She wanted more, needed more, she could feel the buildup coming, slow and steady as she whispered, "Harder."

He quickened his pace, slamming into her, sweat glistened on his back. She matched his movements with her own, the two locked, moving in sync. He then stopped, Holly began to protest when he suddenly flipped her over, pressing his chest against her back, his weight on top of her.

He moved her hair over and put his mouth next to her ear. "Do you know how gorgeous you are?" Holly could not answer him as his left hand snaked underneath her and began to massage her, leaving her breathless. He entered her from behind, going deeper this time. Her hands grabbed onto the blankets and held on as he continued to ride her, her moans of pleasure becoming louder and louder.

"That's it, Holly, come for me, baby." The combination of his hand and his thrusts inside her threw her toward the edge, her body tensed up, and he said roughly, "I want to hear you come this time, don't hold back."

She screamed in ecstasy as he thrusted and came with her, collapsing on top of her. They stayed like that for a moment, his entire body covering hers, their sweat and hair tangled in each other. Then, planting the softest of kisses on her back in between her should blades, he rolled off her, sending chills up her spine as the warmth from his body left her.

With what felt like all her strength, she rolled onto her back and sat up. Her body protested for her to go back to bed and lie in the hazy post coital relaxation. Knowing better, she walked to the bathroom. Washing her hands, she looked into the mirror and saw the face of a woman in complete satisfaction. She now knew the meaning of the phrase *bedroom eyes* as she looked into her own, half open. Her lips and surrounding skin were pink and raw from his stubble as was the nape of her neck and breasts, her hair was a tangled mess of curls. Running her fingers to try and create some semblance of sexy temptress back into her look, she opened the door and saw Luke under the covers, waiting for her. Shyly, she walked over and got under the covers, facing him. He tangled his legs with hers and pulled her closer, chest pressing against hers, and gave her a soft kiss.

"Would you like to sleep in here tonight?"

He answered by giving her another kiss that made Holly's toes curl, she took it as a yes.

Chapter Sixteen

The rest of the night was spent talking, lying in each other's arms, and having sex.

Mind-blowing sex.

By the time they fell asleep, it was well past midnight and half of the box of condoms were history. She fell asleep in his arms right in the middle of the bed. When he woke up, Luke was surprised to see his arm still thrown over her, they really must have worn each other out if they barely moved all night.

He rolled onto his back and stretched, the blood pumping throughout his body again. He looked over at Holly, his movements caused the sheet covering her to pull, revealing her entire backside, and the blood moved down into a certain part of his body again. Just one look at the woman and he could not control himself. He shifted onto his side, coming up behind her and pulled her close when she groaned. He gave a throaty laugh and moved his now fully erect self against her, a sleepy smile appeared on her face, eyes still closed.

She slowly turned over, facing Luke, and proceeded to bury her face in the nape of his neck. "That is one way to wake a girl up."

He held her, gently stroking her bare back with his fingertips, making her snuggle in closer until her breath evened out again. Looking around the room, he took in the strewn clothing, the discarded condoms and wrappers, the top blanket of the bed thrown in a heap on the floor. The sun streamed in through the windows, kissing Holly's beautifully smooth shoulders. He felt like he could stay this way forever, here, in this bed, with her in his arms.

Last night solidified it, he was never letting this girl go. She was funny, beautiful, incredibly sexy, and at least for the next twenty-four hours, only his. His mood dampened slightly as he remembered what was waiting for them back in the city, and his arms instinctively tightened around Holly's body. Picturing the look on Phil's face as he stared at her made Luke's blood boil. He would not let anything happen to her; he would protect her.

A low growl sounded from his stomach. He weighed his options of staying here, lying in blissful peace, or going downstairs and eating, fueling up, for what he hoped would be more of the same as last night. He carefully rolled Holly onto her back and tiptoed out of the room, grabbing a pair of basketball shorts on the way.

He grimaced as he walked into the kitchen. When they went upstairs last night, they stayed there and forgot to clean up after dinner. He started in on the task, gathering all the dishes still outside and loading them in the dishwasher. He wiped down the counters and seeing that it was already ten, made sure the burgers and hotdogs were thawed for later. He poured himself a bowl of cereal and rather than sit inside in silence, took his phone and walked outside to the two-seated rocking chair on the dock. He put on his favorite playlist and ate, slowly rocking back and forth to the music.

Ten minutes later he heard the back door open. Holly wore her bikini from yesterday and walked out toward him. "Mind if I join?"

Luke sat up, making room on the chair for her. She plopped down, draping her legs over his lap, and smiled. "Did you sleep okay?" A small hint of doubt was hidden in her voice. She wasn't just asking about sleep, she was asking about them, how they were today after being together the way they were the day before.

"I slept great. In fact, probably the best sleep I've had in days. Whatever I did to wear me out like that yesterday I should probably do again today, just so I can say I've been well rested after this little get away."

Holly snorted with laughter and rolled her eyes but could not keep a smile off her face. "So we've got the plan for tonight set, what would you like to do today?"

"I say we relax for a bit, make lunch, then maybe take the boat out?"

Holly nodded and swung her legs off him and stood up. "Sounds good. I'll go make the coffee." She walked behind the rocker and put her arms around his shoulders planting a kiss on the cheek before she walked back to the house.

She turned around and called out, "Maybe we can get the hot tub going too? I'm feeling a little sore, might need some warm water for my muscles." Luke smiled, finishing his bowl of cereal and sat there looking out onto the water, feeling completely blissful.

The morning went by quickly. He turned on the hot tub at Holly's request and helped massage some of her sore muscles. It proved to be very difficult to leave the warm water with the jets blowing and Holly wrapped around him, but soon his stomach was growling again. He reluctantly left the hot tub and grilled burgers for the two of them, trying hard to concentrate on the flames in front of him and not the tantalizing woman sitting in the water just a few feet away.

Around one thirty, when the sun was at its highest, they took the boat out. Today, Holly sat in the back of the boat, next to Luke. They drove around the lake a few times, seeming to be the only ones out again. He turned on the radio, both bobbing their heads in time with the music.

She looked at him with a smile and said, "Can't let you dance alone, can I?" Looking at her now, holding a beer, looking out on the water with the wind blowing through her hair, he wished he had a camera to capture her looking this like, beautiful and at ease. The moment ended as he slowed down the boat and she got up and lay down on the cushions.

He decided to anchor in a more secluded area of the lake today, a small inlet surrounded by trees. Even though no one else seemed to be out on the lake today, he wanted to assure complete privacy for the two of them. He went and lay down on the cushions opposite her and closed his eyes, taking in the sun. A soft noise came from the floor, he looked down and saw Holly's bikini top. She was lying on her back with her hands above her head, pushing her chest up. Her eyes were closed, but there was a hint of a smile on her face. She knew he was looking at her and the effect it would have on him.

A small breeze came in, and her nipples hardened instantly. Luke's swim trunks began to feel uncomfortably tight. "You know—" His voice came out a bit rougher than he would've liked. "—it's very hot; you're going to need to put some more sunscreen on."

She opened her eyes and turned her head toward

him, a wicked glint hidden beneath an innocent façade. "Can you help me put some on?"

Luke sat up and looked around making sure no one was on land as he got up and grabbed the sunscreen bottle. He gently lifted her head, placing it on his lap as he squirted some lotion out into his hand. Her eyes were shut again, but her breathing had become shallower, a sign she was getting excited. He slowly lowered his palms to each breast and began to massage them. She lifted her chest, pushing them into his hands as he caressed her. Moving his fingers toward her nipples, he began to lightly pinch them as a soft noise escaped Holly's lips, her head rolling so her face was against his stomach. Her hot breath on his abdomen sent waves of pleasure directly to his groin as it continued to grow. Maybe placing her head on his lap was not a good move…but it gave Luke an idea.

Once the lotion was all rubbed in, he immediately took his hands off her and scooted off the bench earning a whimper of protest from Holly.

"It's just so hot; I'm gonna take a dip." Going to the back of the boat he eased himself into the water, unable to jump with a throbbing erection, and spun around. He quickly shimmied out of his trunks and threw them on the boat. "There, that's better."

Holly pursed her lips and lifted an eyebrow. Looking around to confirm no eyes were on her, she stood up so that her body wasn't shielded by the boat's edge and removed her bottoms. She walked to the back of the boat and slowly dipped her body into the water. Once completely submerged, she swam her way over to a waiting Luke.

Without saying a word, she put her arms around his

neck and wrapped her legs around his waist. Her center brushed against his hard shaft and his hiss of pleasure was cut short as she kissed him, slow and sensually. Luke cupped her bottom and lifted her slightly out of the water so that he was face to face with her chest.

"How are you doing that? Don't you need to keep us floating?"

Luke gave a throaty laugh. "I can touch the ground here." He took one pert breast into his mouth and sucked hard. Holly cried out in pleasure, her nails dug into his shoulder, and she squeezed her thighs, rubbing against him. He placed his hand against her back to hold her in place as he switched his attention to her other breast, gently using his teeth to graze her nipple. A sound of pleasure escaped her lips and echoed off the wall of trees. She pulled his hair hard, separating his mouth from her chest, claiming it with her lips. She kissed him hard, moving her hips back and forth on top of his erection. The feel of the warm water mixed with her body on top started to bring Luke to the edge. The hand holding her shifted so that his fingers found her opening and dipped inside. Her hand snaked down in between their bodies and grasped him. She moved with his strokes now, the water around them rippling excitedly.

She stopped kissing him, closed her eyes, and leaned her head back. Luke watched as his fingers brought her closer to climax, her breasts bouncing up and down out of the water. He closed his eyes and let the sensations take over, finishing, with her joining just a few moments later.

Leaning forward, she placed her forehead against his, both of their breathing ragged. He opened his eyes and stared into hers seeing no amusement, no lightheartedness, just pure emotion. He was sure his eyes mirrored hers. All was silent except for the gentle lapping of water around their shoulders.

Holly was the first to break the silence. "I think…" She stopped herself, heaving a sigh. She slowly let go of Luke, much to his disappointment, and waded away. Her tone changed, and she raised her eyebrows playfully. "I think we should get our suits on before someone comes by. I was probably a bit too loud."

"Holly wait, I—"

"Can you turn around while I get back onto the boat?"

"Yeah." He turned and listened to the splash made as Holly raised herself back onto the boat. He didn't know what she was about to say, but he knew that if she hadn't said something, he would've blurted it out.

I love you.

The words had been bubbling up in his chest, after a release like that it felt like a natural thing to think, to say. He had never said it to anyone he dated but was sure that a proclamation like that usually happened later in a relationship, not a few weeks in. And he definitely did not want to scare her off and ruin things. No, it was good that they go back to playful, at least for the time being.

"Okay you can turn around."

Holly was back in her bikini and gave him a small, embarrassed smile. "Thanks, that just wouldn't have been a flattering angle for you to see."

Luke waded over to the edge of the boat, lifting himself up. "That's okay; I understand. Let's drive around a bit and cool off." He slipped his trunks back on and passed Holly to go toward the driver's seat, pausing to give her a kiss on the cheek. She grabbed a few beers, handing one to Luke, and the two spent the rest of the afternoon drinking and enjoying each other's company.

Once they finally got back to the dock, Luke felt drained. After tying up the boat he turned to Holly who was gathering her things. "I think I'm going to lie down for an hour, recharge before dinner."

She continued to gather their items off the boat and responded without looking up, "I'm going to grill dinner tonight so lie down for as long as you want."

He nodded and began to walk back to the house.

"Hey, Luke?"

He turned to see Holly, now looking at him. "Today was great. Thanks for driving me around." She smiled, and he felt his spirits lift. Smiling back, he continued up to the house and his awaiting bed.

****

Holly closed the back door behind her, dropping a heap of towels onto the floor, and flopped on the couch. She was exhausted from being out in the sun all day and from the...activities she and Luke did. Turning onto her back, she stared up at the ceiling. At this very moment, he was sleeping right above her. Part of her wanted to crawl into bed with him and nap in his arms for an hour. She knew that if they were in a bed together, they weren't getting out of it for a long time, and it certainly would not be restful. Sighing in frustration, she remembered the moment in the water together.

I think I'm falling for you.

It was what she almost said but ended up chickening out. She didn't want to scare him, but she had felt overcome with emotion. Looking into his eyes after sharing that intimate moment, it felt right. But she got scared. Scared of freaking him out, of scaring him off, of this all being over, and she didn't want that to happen. She was not usually someone who held herself back when it came to telling the truth and saying how she felt so she felt out of her element.

What's done is done

She got up from the couch.

If the time comes again, I won't be a baby and I'll just say it and whatever happens will happen.

She walked silently up the stairs into the master bedroom, wanting to shower and wash the lake out of her hair. Luke was sprawled on his stomach, his tanned skin stood out against the stark white sheets. The image recalled the myth of a curious Psyche creeping in to sneak a peek at a sleeping Cupid, she remembered the word used, "angelic". It popped into her mind as she gazed down at the sleeping Luke. She so wanted to run her fingers through his curls, feel his stubble on the nape of her neck but also needed to not smell like suntan lotion and a lake. Shaking herself out of her small daydream, she went into the bathroom.

She was going to miss this shower when she got back to the city. They had to go back tomorrow. Back to her terrible water pressure, back to the close living quarters, back to Phil. The bottle of conditioner slipped from her grasp, and she jumped at the sound making a little squeak then immediately clamped her hands over her mouth. Her eyes shot over through the glass wall of the shower to the door, worried she had woken up the beautiful man on the other side of the door. It remained closed, and she relaxed putting her hands against the shower wall and dropping her head, letting the water run down her back.

The tears that came surprised her, but she did not try

to stop them. She let herself cry, her tears mixing with the water. She wrapped her arms around herself, letting the water draw her hair over her face. She did not want to go back home for fear of what would happen. She thought of Phil, of his staring, thought of Kate, she thought of Jennifer Lawler, wherever she was, and of Lisa sitting in their apartment, sad and alone. She was thinking so much she did not hear the bathroom door open. She felt the rush of cold from the glass door opening and looked up to see Luke, in his naked perfection, coming into the shower with her. Neither of them said a word as he put his arms around her, and she continued to cry. He stroked her back as she wrapped her arms around his waist, burying her head in his chest.

"Phil?"

She nodded, and they went back to their silence. After a while he grabbed the bottle of conditioner she had dropped, squirted it into his hands, and started to run them through her hair. Holly grabbed the soap and lathered it in her hands, running them up and down his body. They cleaned each other, the whole time not speaking. When they were done, they dried off and found some fluffy robes to wrap themselves in. They lay on the bed wrapped up in each other, watching TV.

Holly was thankful he did not push her, did not ask her anything. He seemed to know there was nothing to say to make her feel better, but he did not need to. Him simply being there was enough for her.

The hours passed, and soon both of their stomachs were growling. Holly sat up and ran her fingers through her hair. "Food?"

He grunted in agreement. "Food."

They dressed and made their way downstairs. He put

on some music, and the two cooked dinner, side by side as the music blasted. Once everything was done, they sat at the patio table and ate. Holly was the first to speak. "Hear me out. We stay here forever. Kate and Tommy move here, too. They could bring all of our stuff."

Unphased, Luke said, "I'm not hating that idea, but once winter comes, you'll regret everything. Plus, think about the hassle of changing your address on all your records and information. Plus, we'd need a car to get around up here."

She pretended to consider this. "I see what you're saying but also I wasn't listening, and I think my plan is still perfect."

"The sad fact," he continued after he swallowed his food, "is that we will be returning tomorrow. If the officers' estimate of a few days is accurate, we've still got some time before we hear about the blood on that shirt. So, we go back and live our lives which now involve each other a lot more so you'll be safe."

Holly furrowed her brow. "Um you'll be safe too since I'll be around you as well. You're involved just as much as me."

Luke stopped chewing. "I'm not the one getting stared at, Holly. I know what he's thinking and I just…" He balled his fists, and his knuckles turned white. Holly placed a hand over his.

He nodded. "Let's not talk about it until tomorrow?"

Once they finished eating, Holly grabbed his hand and her drink and led them to the two-seated rocking chair stationed on the dock. The sun was setting as they settled down, Luke's arm laid across the top of the seat as they rocked peacefully, sipping on their beers, looking at the wonderful view.

"I think," he began slowly, "these have been the best two days of my entire year. A close third being the day I moved into my new apartment."

"And met me?" Holly teased.

"Well…yeah." She looked up as an air of seriousness invaded the conversation. "You're pretty great if you didn't know it."

Holly turned back to the view and snuggled her head into his chest. "I know." She felt his chest move with laughter, and she smiled. "You are too you know."

"I know and that opinion will be reinforced when I tell you I bought things to make s'mores."

She bolted up, eyes wide with excitement. "What the hell are we doing here? Go build me a fire!"

The two cleaned up dinner, built the bonfire, and toasted marshmallows while sitting on one of the cushy loveseats. Holly couldn't remember the last time she did something like this, sit around a fire, be outside, snuggled up with a beautiful man. She would have been happy to spend the whole night out there, talking and gazing at the flames had Luke not started kissing her neck, letting his hand wander below the blanket.

The rest of the night was spent in a similar fashion to the one before. Once the fire was out, they went upstairs and did not leave the room the rest of the night. Instead of the fast paced, wild passion that had taken hold of them the previous evening, this time was slower and more intimate. Holly's feelings for him heightened as he made love to her, helped lull her into a deep sleep.

The next morning, they tidied up the house. Washing the sheets and towels they used, they locked up and started their journey back to the city. As they drove farther away from the lake house, Holly found her good mood staying behind with it. Thoughts of the missing girls started to flood her mind as they drove.

Luke kept looking over, trying to start the conversation up, but she kept dropping it. Finally, while waiting in line for lunch at a drive through window, he turned to her. "Turn it off."

She was confused. "Huh?"

"Turn your brain off. I can see it working hard, and it's putting you in a terrible mood. We just had a couple fantastic days together. Don't let that get overshadowed in your head."

Holly shook her head. "I know, I can't help it. But yes, I agree, we did have a great few days."

"And..." he continued, now looking slightly uncomfortable. "It doesn't have to stop now that we're going home. I mean, we're still going to—I mean, I want to see you—um—more or still—um consistently."

He was looking everywhere but her, trying to find the words and she found it utterly adorable. "Yes, we are still going to see each other, Luke. You're not getting rid of me that easily."

"So, we're dating." He said it as a statement, but the tone was a questioning one.

She was unable to keep the amusement off her face. "I would like to be dating you."

"Good, because I would like to be dating you, too."

The clarification of the relationship put Holly in a better mood for the remainder of the drive. As the skyline came into view and the thoughts about what awaited her entered her mind again, she reached and grabbed Luke's free hand and squeezed, he squeezed back, and she felt more prepared to return to real life.

Chapter Seventeen

Holly walked into her apartment and dropped her bags. "Hello?"

The sound of feet pounding the floor grew louder as Kate rounded the corner coming into view, a relieved look on her face. "You're home!" She threw her arms around her, giving her a tight hug.

Abruptly she let go and led her to the couch. "We have a lot to discuss. First, I want to tell you all about my trip, and Ben says hi. Then I need to scream at you for being stupid and doing something so dangerous. Then you are going to tell me all about your trip and give me details because if you two were away together I know that something happened, and I want to hear about it."

"I uh, yes. Give me a moment, I just need to think about how you got that all out in one breath."

She learned about her friend's drive, getting lost, the weird place they stayed, and the sexual details that she didn't ask for, but of course wanted to know. Kate, in turn, learned about the dinner date that had led to them tailing Phil, about the shirt, the break in, the revenge break in conducted by Holly, and finally the lake house. It took her a good twenty minutes to tell her the whole story and, by the time she was done, Kate was leaning back against the couch cushions, mouth open and brow furrowed.

"That is a lot of information."

Holly nodded her head numbly. "Tell me about it."

Her roommate looked at her, dazed. "I just don't understand how you've managed to become the target of a crazy man's wrath and also get a boyfriend within the span of a week."

Holly gave Kate's arm a light smack, then stood. "I don't either, but what I do know is that you and I are going to be on high alert for the time being, okay? We're using all the locks and keeping our eyes peeled. Now I am going to go unpack and catch up on my stories." She turned on her heel and marched into her room with a flourish, earning an eye roll from Kate.

After dumping her bag into the laundry basket, Holly quickly sat down and opened her laptop. She checked her email then switched over to the *Murder for Your Thoughts* homepage. The page loaded and she saw the familiar black and yellow banner at the top but instead of a new story there was the word *Update* in big bold letters laying over the previous week's story.

There has been an update in the Missing Ladies of Lakeview Case that I wrote about a few weeks ago. Sadly, it is not happy information. Another woman has gone missing. Her name is Jennifer Lawler and much like the other victims was a woman between the ages of 25 and 35 and lived in the Lakeview neighborhood of Chicago. Jennifer's roommate, Lisa Canton, was interviewed by police and learned new information that could be helpful to future ladies.

Lisa left the apartment, swearing she had locked the door behind her, with Jennifer inside. After police investigated the lock, they found tiny scratches on the outside of the mechanism leading experts to believe that it was unlocked with a set of picking tools. Police say they are now going back to examine each of the locks of the victims to confirm the theory.

If you know anything, see anything, or are suspicious of anything, call the police. We can help find these ladies and catch the monster responsible. Stay safe, my Chicago friends.

As she re-read the update, a chill crept up her spine. She knew it was Phil who was responsible for breaking into her apartment, proven by the fact that she found the shirt in his trunk. She knew that he could pick a lock and she knew, or technically suspected, that he was to blame for all the disappearances, but to see R.J. write and confirm at least a portion of her theory was upsetting. Not that the situation wasn't real before, but now…she instinctively looked out the window she sat in front of, scanning the street before her.

As usual her window showed people going about their day, people walking dogs, people standing—her eyes locked on a figure down the street, partially hidden by a tree. She squinted as she watched the unmoving figure. Was it just her imagination or was that person…looking at her? She leaned over her desk, moving closer to the window, trying to make out any discernable features, but all she could see was a blurry shape.

Suddenly, the figure moved around the tree, slowly walking in her direction. The closer it got, the more in focus it became, and Holly made out a faded blue baseball hat. She gasped moving away from the window. Immediately, she closed her blinds and sat down on the floor, out of view from the now covered window. She hugged her knees to her chest, attempting to control her breathing.

After ten minutes, she worked up the courage to peek out of the corner of her window. She crawled to the wall and lifted the blinds an inch, scanning the street. The figure in the blue hat was gone. A relieved sigh escaped her, but she made the decision to keep the blinds down for the rest of the day, just in case.

She tried to relax. Out in the living room she sat with Kate, who was watching TV, still technically on vacation until the next day. They filled the hours watching multiple blonde actresses fall in love with handsome dark-haired men, while eating cheese and crackers and sipping glass after glass of wine. Day had turned into night when Holly's phone chimed with a text from Luke.

–I know I just spent two days with U but I kind of miss U—

Holly smiled and responded.

–I kinda miss U 2. I'm going to have to buy another pillow since I don't have you to spoon me tonight—

Luke's reply was instant.

–We can fix that U know. I don't live that far away. Come over?–

She considered the invitation and then looked over as her friend snuggled into the couch, her feet pressed up next to hers.

–While I would usually jump at that chance, I want to spend time with Kate tonight but how about tomorrow night?—

–I understand. Can't wait—

Even though so much had happened between them, she still felt the butterflies in her stomach at the anticipation of spending the night with him. She blew out a breath, and Kate looked over. "Loverboy texting you?"

She smiled and nodded. "Gross."

They both laughed and returned their attention to the screen.

****

The next day came, and the household fell back into its normal routine. Kate worked non-stop while Holly did tasks here and there, taking care to remain inside and away from the windows just for peace of mind. As night fell, she got ready to go over to Luke's and found herself getting nervous.

While they had already spent a lot of time together, Holly still agonized over which cute pair of pajamas to wear, whether she should shave her legs even though she had just a few days ago, and even if she should put on a tiny bit of makeup? She had never been on a date where the primary goal was to literally sleep with each person, and it felt funny to get ready for one.

Of course, Kate came in and gave her opinion on everything—even lending her a silky top and shorts set after she rejected Holly's idea of makeup with the argument of *did she want him to see remnants of makeup on his pillowcase the next morning*? As she left, she asked Kate to lock the door behind her and that she would see her in the morning.

Luke answered and raised his eyebrows when he saw Holly in the silky two-piece set.

"Why didn't you bring these to the lake house?" He stepped aside and let her in.

"Because I didn't get the chance to wear pjs for the last two nights." She raised up on her tip toes and kissed him on the lips, she felt him smile against her mouth. "Tommy still out of town?"

Luke grinned and nodded. "We've got the whole place to ourselves." He bent down giving her another kiss, this one longer and steamier, making her feel almost dizzy with desire.

"How about we put on a movie and make out on the couch for a while?"

Luke nodded his head vigorously at her suggestion and practically pulled Holly's arm off as he led her quickly to the couch. "Let's go hardcore high school and put on a scary movie."

She giggled. They landed on a cheesy 80's horror to put on as they snuggled into each other's arms against the couch. Holly rolled her head up toward him, studying his features. Feeling her eyes on him, he smiled down at her asking, "You okay?"

Holly nodded. "Kind of in this weird head space, but I'm doing okay. You?"

Luke shrugged. "I think I'm in the same space, especially being back from the paradise that was Wisconsin."

She reached out her arm pulling him closer, he leaned back so his head lay on her chest as she stroked his hair. He shifted more, and the pair ended up lying side by side, facing each other on the couch, his long body hanging over the edge. His left hand lazily ran up and down her thigh where it rested on top of his hip.

"You're missing the 80's gore by facing this way and not the TV," she joked. He silently smiled, continuing to gaze at her. Rather than let herself feel embarrassed at his blatant staring, she ran her hand over the stubble on his cheek.

"I'm sorry for everything that's happened." His voice came out soft, almost a whisper.

Holly gave him a sleepy smile. "Me, too. Except for the meeting you part."

He mirrored her expression. "Yeah, the 'you' part has been good. You know what I realized?" She shook her head. "Once things get back to normal, we can stop being interrupted." Her confused expression led him to continue. "Except for the lake house, every time you and I have been together, it's been interrupted somehow, but that piece of shi—"

"Shhhhh." She cut him off, putting a finger on his lips to silence him and then let her finger trace the outline of his mouth and down his chin, scratching his stubble. "I didn't realize that."

Her attention went back to her fingers where they still stroked his cheek. She felt so happy here in his arms, but a tiny voice in the back of her head kept nagging her. Maybe this was all circumstantial, that he wasn't on the same page as her. Drawing in a breath, she decided to tackle the doubt head on.

"You're not…you're not going to be bored with me when things settle down, will you?"

Luke looked visibly taken aback and said in a matter-of-fact tone, "Absolutely not."

She kept her gaze on her finger, refusing to meet his eyes, the confidence she had in asking the question evaporated in an instant, and embarrassment took over.

"Look at me." His voice was still gentle, but his tone was firm, giving Holly cause to slowly draw her eyes back to his. "I'm crazy about you. The moment I saw you, I was a goner."

Her chest swelled with emotion as he continued. "I've wanted to say something since the lake actually." He paused, taking her hand which was stroking his cheek and turning it, planting a kiss on the inside of her wrist. It was such an intimate act, one that made Holly's insides wake up. Her body stirring in anticipation, only Luke could awaken those feelings at a time like this, and without meaning to at that. He looked up at her, his green eyes making her feel like the whole world was on pause.

"I think you wanted to say something too, but you played it cool, so I just followed your lead."

He planted another kiss now higher on the inside of her arm, again sending an electric current straight to her core and zinging through the rest of her body. His eyes locked on hers, and she knew this was the time to say what she felt, but as she looked into his eyes, she got that foreign feeling of fear.

What if the opposite happened to her? What if she ended up feeling bored of him? What if all this excitement and energy between them was just a product of their surroundings? She would not want to hurt him, to cause this man any pain, he was too good, he didn't deserve it.

In the silence, he planted another kiss on her wrist, and Holly decided rather than responding verbally, she would just show him her feelings. She yanked his head toward her and lost herself in the kiss, and he responded in kind. She shifted so now she lay on top of him and soon enough she found herself straddling him, her attention fully on where his hands were going when all of a sudden, she heard a muted shout.

Pulling away, she caught her breath. "Did you hear that?" Luke's attention was dragged away from feeling what was under her silky camisole and looked at her with lazy eyes.

"I did not, but whatever it was we should ignore it and get back to this." Holly shot him an amused look and looked around for the remote.

"I'm sure it was the movie." She grabbed the controller and clicked the mute button, turning her attention back to him. Another moment later they heard a loud thud followed by a crash. Both Holly and Luke's eyes flew open, his grip on her waist tightened.

"You heard something that time, right?"

He nodded. They stayed still, eyes glued to the door, until they heard the loud bang of a door being slammed, a door that sounded like it was right next door. He quickly moved Holly off his lap and said in a low, terse voice, "Stay here."

He got up and looked through the peep hole. Seeming to have seen nothing he moved back and opened the door, moving into the hallway cautiously. "Holly. Call the police."

Scared, she grabbed her cell phone and ran into the hallway as she dialed nine one one. She heard a voice on the other end but could not speak as she saw the door to her apartment open.

Luke, hearing the questioning voice on the other end and seeing a scared Holly, grabbed the phone from her. "Yes, I'd like to report a break in." He proceeded to give them the address.

Her voice finally seemed to work. "Where's Kate?"

Luke looked at her sharply and back to the door. Still holding the phone to his ear, he slowly pushed her door open with the back of his hand and stepped into the apartment, she followed closely behind.

"Kate?"

When there was no answer. She looked around but nothing seemed out of place. She slowly walked past Luke and checked her room. The door was open but again, nothing was disturbed.

"Kate?" She called again, passing the untouched living room arriving at Kate's closed door, light streaming through the crack at the bottom. She slowly pushed open the door and gasped. The room was in disarray. Her lamp, which lived on her nightstand was on the ground, the shade unattached. Some books had been thrown around, clothing lay haphazardly on the ground, but the most disturbing part was the bed. The sheets were every which way, and the pillows were scattered, and Kate wasn't in it.

Holly immediately ran to the kitchen, flung the back door open, and went on the porch, tears in her eyes looking across the way. The light was off in the second-window apartment.

Phil was not in.

Chapter Eighteen

It was not just Officers Shane and Martinez who responded to the emergency call this time. After realizing Kate was not in the apartment, Luke told the operator that not only was there a break-in but likely a kidnapping as well.

After hanging up, he led a sobbing Holly into the hallway and held her while they waited for the authorities to arrive. The heaving sobs subsided, but a constant stream of tears ran down her face. While needing to keep it together for Holly's sake, inside he dealt with a plethora of emotions.

Leaving to grab a sweatshirt with the intention to cover her up before the police arrived, he took the time to take a deep breath and sort through the plethora of thoughts and emotions running through his head.

He was scared that something like this could happen with them only right next door; relieved Holly had been out of the apartment; guilt over his relief that it was Kate who was missing. Overall, it was the rising anger inside. If he ever got his hands on Phil, he was sure there would be two arrests made that day.

When the police did arrive, Officer Martinez, now a too familiar sight, ushered the couple into Luke's apartment while the handful of other officers made their way into Kate's room, now considered a crime scene.

Still overwhelmed, Holly sat with her head in her

hands while Luke relayed most of the story. She lifted her head as he finished talking, tears still streamed down her face. "Have you tested the shirt?"

Martinez closed his notebook. "Not yet but I promise it will move up on the list. We're going to do everything we can to find your friend."

Her voice became low with a slight edge. "You'll be taking him in for questioning, right?"

"You can be sure we're going to do some digging."

She stood abruptly. "Digging *and* questioning, right? I mean, this isn't about some fricking theory anymore, Kate is gone." Her voice rose. "She is gone, and it's my fault because I provoked that monster. It should be me who's missing; we need to find her now."

Luke rose to his feet. He held onto her shoulder, scared she might actually lash out at the officer.

Officer Martinez took her hand, a move that surprised Luke for the personal touch. "I'll bring him in for questioning." Gently dropping her hand, he glanced at Luke's hand still firmly in place. "Listen, I believe you both. This guy has been acting suspicious and aggressive. If I don't do things by the book, and it ends up being him, he could go free. Do you understand?"

They both nodded sullenly, Holly stepped back and wrapped Luke's arm around her. He gave her a quick, hopefully comforting, squeeze.

Martinez looked into the hallway, then back at them. "You'll be able to go back and sleep in your room if you want, you just can't enter her bedroom. However, I personally think you should stay somewhere else tonight. Do you have somewhere to go?"

Luke answered for her, saying, "She'll be staying with me until Kate returns."

Just then, Officer Shane entered the room. "We just want to let you know that it looks like he picked the initial lock, then broke the door down, breaking the two newer locks you installed since our earlier visit. There was nothing you could have done short of getting an in-home security system, so don't beat yourself up." He looked at Holly who gave a teary nod. "Since you've had a few issues before, we're going to keep a patrol on your street for the next few nights just to monitor the comings and goings."

They all nodded, as the officers started to leave. Luke led Holly back to the couch then turned and followed the officers outside. "Wait, please."

When the officers turned, he asked, "Will you please contact me when you bring him in for questioning? I know it's probably not the usual thing to do, but I feel like shooting me a discreet text is better than having her," —he gestured back to his apartment—"call in to the station a bunch and jam up the phone lines because you know that's exactly what's going to happen."

The officers shared a considering look. Shane pursed his lips and turned his head as Martinez gave Luke a quick nod.

"Thank you, so much."

The men said their goodnights and left, Luke took out his cell phone and started dialing, Tommy picked up on the second ring. "Hey. I hope you haven't forgotten about me just because you've been in the throes of ecstasy with your new girlfriend."

He let out a dark laugh. "Yeah I *was* in the throes." He quickly related the events of the past few hours to his friend who stayed silent the entire time.

When he was done, Tommy took a moment to

respond. "I leave for a few days, and you go and let our neighbor get kidnapped?"

"Tommy, now is not the time…"

A nervous chuckle came over the phone. "I know, I'm sorry. Is Holly okay? Are you okay? It sounds like you're really acting as her leaning post here."

Luke slowly paced around the small courtyard while talking. "Well, of course, I don't know…. I don't know anything. I feel like she's going to need a while, she just keeps crying which like, why wouldn't she? Me? I don't know, I just…I keep thinking if our places were switched and if it were you who was taken…" He couldn't finish the sentence; he didn't trust himself to not become emotional.

Tommy's tone gentled. "Hey, I know, bud, but I'm not. I'm okay and you and Holly are okay. And Kate…hopefully will be okay. Plus, you know, no one in their right mind would want to kidnap me, I'm not pretty like you." He paused, turning serious again. "Do you want me to come back? Maybe I can help in some way?"

"No, I'd rather you stay there until all this craziness kind of calms down. We've got police here on the street watching the building. I just… I love you, man, okay?"

"I love you too, bud. Text me with updates, okay, and let me know if I can do anything?"

Back in his apartment, he came upon Holly, silently crying, staring off into the distance, and something inside him broke. He sat down next to her, moving her onto his lap, her arms automatically swung around his neck as she sobbed on his shoulder.

"Cry all you want, I'm here for you." It was all he could say as he stroked her back and held her tight.

After a while, the tears stopped and she looked up,

sniffling. Her eyes were puffy, her lashes wet, eyes glistening with the possibility of more tears, and Luke had to tamp down the anger he felt for the man responsible for making her cry once more.

She sniffled. "I'm tired."

Luke shifted her, putting one arm under her knees and the other tightening against her back, and stood with her in his arms, carrying her to his bedroom. He pushed the door open with his foot and placed her gently on the bed. He left the room only to turn off the lights outside and double check that they were locked in for the night. Stopping under the doorframe he looked back at her, curled up in the middle of his bed, still wearing his sweatshirt. She looked so small, a gray dot in a sea of navy sheets.

His room was not really the comforting space Holly was used to. His eyes did a sweep of the room, his weights were out of the way in the corner, his desk sat against the wall, papers astray on it, a few random posters pinned to the wall with random colored safety pins. It was now that he wished he'd invested in things like nice blankets, frames for his wall art, and maybe a broom to sweep all the dust bunnies out from under the bed. Luke thought for a moment and ran to the living room, coming back with a lighter and candle from the front room.

With Holly silently watching him from her position on the bed, Luke placed the candle on the nightstand next to her side of the bed, lit it, turned off the lights, and went and lay in the bed next to her. He placed his body up against her, forming a protective shell around her.

"Why did you grab a candle?" Her question was muffled by the hands balled in front of her mouth.

"You have them scattered around your entire apartment. I thought maybe this would make you feel a tiny bit better."

She chuckled and rotated, facing Luke in the bed, and proceeded to bury her head in the crook of his neck.

"Thank you." He held her close, and they stayed that way until they fell asleep.

Luke woke up the next morning alone in the bed. Panic set in as he bolted up and ran out of his room and right into Holly, who was carrying a mug of coffee and talking on the phone. She skittered out of the way balancing the steaming mug letting only a little bit of coffee dribble over the edge. "Allie, please just stay where you are. I don't want you coming here right now, everything is so up in the air and not to mention dangerous...yes I love you too...No I'm not alone, as I said, I am with Luke." She mouthed *I'm sorry* to a still startled Luke and handed him the dripping mug. "Look, Al, I gotta go, but I promise I will keep you updated on everything...yes, I also promise I will ask you to come if I need you, okay? Okay. Love you too. Bye." She hung up the phone and gestured to the steaming mug in his hand.

"That would've been a bad way to start the day, coffee burns on your chest? No thank you."

She'd taken off his sweatshirt and was back to wearing just the silk set, her hair tousled. A first impression would make you think she had a good night's sleep but looking closer, Luke saw the circles under her eyes and the puffiness that had yet to go down after last night's events.

"I was worried when I woke up and you weren't there. How are you feeling this morning?"

"I made some coffee; I couldn't sleep anymore. I was going to go shower, change, and come back with my laptop."

Luke put the mug down on his dresser on the inside of the doorway. "You were gonna go back there without telling me? I don't think that's a good idea."

Holly's features showed first confusion and then annoyance. "Well, what do you suggest? I have to go get my things, continue with my life, isn't that what I'm supposed to do?"

Luke put his hands up in defense. "Hey, I just meant maybe I can go with you, I'll wait on the couch while you do your thing. I just don't want you to be in there alone right now."

Holly, still visibly annoyed, averted her eyes. "Fine, whatever. Can we go now?"

Grabbing his mug, keys, phone, and throwing on a shirt, he walked across the hall with Holly who went immediately into the bathroom, practically slamming the door. Luke knew she wasn't mad at him but at the situation, he would be too if their roles were reversed. He just wished there was more he could do to help her.

He walked to the window and opened the blinds, giving him a glimpse of the street. A cop car was parked a few spots east and people walked up and down the block, going about their days. He thought how lucky they all were, to be living a normal life. Lost in thought, he did not hear the shower shut off or the door open and was surprised when he heard Holly shout, "Get away from there."

He turned to see a dripping wet Holly, wrapped in a towel, standing in the hallway, steam wafting from the now open door behind her. She sped over to the window and grabbed the cord, pulling the blinds shut.

"I was looking out the window, what's wrong?"

"Do you want him looking in here?" she shrieked. "He could be out there right now, knowing we're here."

"Holly, the cops are out there right now. Phil isn't there."

She turned and stomped back to her bedroom and yelled over her shoulder. "Didn't stop him the other day from creeping on me."

"What?" His voice came out louder than intended. He followed into her room, pushing the door open with a loud smack. She jumped and spun around, the anger now gone from her eyes replaced with uncertainty. "I'm not sure it was him, but I saw someone looking at me through the window the other day. He was far enough that I couldn't get a good look, but I'm pretty sure I saw a blue hat."

Luke crossed the room with such speed, it caused Holly to back up against the wall still gripping the towel around her. His hands thrown up in frustration, he yelled, "Why didn't you tell me about this sooner?"

A flash of fear came into Holly's eyes, and he quickly stepped back, the last thing she needed was another person to be afraid of. "I...I didn't know if it was him and I had just read an update on the blog so I...I don't know I thought maybe I imagined it? I...I just..." She bent her head down, bringing it back up to show tears in her eyes. "I guess I just wanted to be wrong, for all of this to be over."

They stood silent for several long moments. Finally, he asked, "Have you kept anything else from me?"

"No."

"Okay, get dressed."

Luke left the room, sitting back down on her couch, avoiding eye contact. He sipped his coffee, attempting to maintain a calm demeanor. She stood, rooted to the spot for another moment looking at him, then finally went into her room, closing the door.

He focused on his breathing trying to figure out what their next steps were but kept circling back to the fact that she kept this from him.

Thinking back, she neglected to say anything to him about her first encounter with Phil as well. Luke was still upset about how close she had come to being discovered in his apartment when she went to fetch the shirt. He was still in this cycle of thoughts when she stepped out of her room looking apologetic. She had thrown her hair up in a wet bun and wore workout capri leggings with a gray tank top, holding her closed laptop at her side.

"Okay, I'm ready." Her voice was quiet, full of worry. He got up, still avoiding her eyes, and walked out of her apartment, back across the hall. She followed, closing his front door and leaning back against it. "Luke, listen…"

"No, you listen." He spun around on his heel, cutting her off. "I am not going away, okay? I will let you use me to vent and to yell at because you're scared, and this situation sucks. But when you purposefully leave me out, not tell me things, put yourself in danger, that's when I'm going to get mad. You cannot do that and expect me to just forgive you and move on. You have to trust me with things, you can't just tell me half the information and expect me to be okay with finding out he's spying on you later. Do you understand what I would do if something happened to you? Do you understand what I would have done if that had been you last night?"

His voice broke and he stopped yelling, running his hands through his curls and over his eyes. All the feelings and emotions from last night erupted and just as suddenly, he was drained. He fell back onto the couch, unable to stand anymore, and placed a hand over his eyes, calming down. He felt the cushions next to him sink and a smaller hand place itself on his thigh.

"I'm so sorry, Luke." He opened his eyes and found Holly at his side, looking remorseful. "I should've told you. I promise from now on to keep you in the loop in case anything happens."

Luke snorted. "For the foreseeable future I will be glued to you, so you don't have to worry about that."

Holly leaned back a little, her eyes narrowed. "You can't be next to me every hour of every day, Luke. At some point we aren't going to be around each other."

"Not if I can help it."

She shook her head and grabbed her laptop. "Too bad, I'm going home." She made her way to the door but Luke, springing up from the couch, beat her there and stood in front of her.

"Holly, please—" Panic now replaced anger. "Please don't go, I don't want you to be alone. I don't want anything to happen to you."

Her features relaxed. "This is getting to be crazy. I think maybe we need a little space."

She reached past him and turned the knob, pushing the door open but Luke kept his feet rooted in place. "Holly, please, I…"

He stopped talking as he watched her face go from annoyance to fear. He swiveled, following her gaze. Taped to the door was a white piece of paper, folded in half. Luke dropped his arm, allowing her to reach around to grab the note. With hands shaking only slightly, she opened the paper, read the message, and looked up.

"What does it say?"

She handed him the note.

You take my things, I take yours.

Chapter Nineteen

Holly didn't cry, not this time.

She'd wept while she spoke to Kate's parents on the phone, then with her own parents and Allie. She bawled with Luke, on Luke, in Luke's bed and, frankly, felt she was all cried out for the time being.

Now all she felt was rage as she marched outside to the police car parked on her street, Luke following a few paces behind. She knocked on the window and waited patiently as it rolled down to reveal two officers, a man and a woman, sitting with pleasant expressions on their faces.

"Miss Harrison, what can we do for you?"

"Have you been watching people entering and leaving my building?"

They looked at each other and back at her in a slightly condescending way. "Of course."

She held up the folded note. "Then you'll be able to tell me who taped this to my door."

The two officers immediately got out of their car and looked over the note. "Miss, no one had entered or exited until you two came out here."

A look of concern was shared between them, and Holly felt fear jump back into her. She looked at Luke, who was staring back at their building, arms crossed over his chest, lost in thought.

"When are you taking him in for questioning?"

Neither officer responded to the question. The female officer used the walkie-talkie to notify her superior while the male placed the note in a bag and sealed it.

Frustrated, Holly walked over to Luke who spoke without taking his eyes off the apartment. "He must've crawled over onto our balcony, gone through your apartment, and then taped it to the door. How else would he have done it?"

"Listen," she whispered so as not to be overheard by the police. "None of the other girls have been found which leads me to believe Phil's killed them. But, in all the articles I've read about him, he's never left a note or anything afterward. This makes me think Kate's still alive."

"I think so, too," he said. "And I think he's keeping her in that storage unit."

Her eyes went wide. Of course, why else would he have a unit that was so close? After breaking into his apartment, she knew that he had a lot of space but not a lot of items filling it.

She touched his arm. "We've got to do something."

The female officer ended her call then, with a grim look on her face, signaled Holly over. "We're going to bring this in for fingerprints. If it matches, then we'll be able to take your neighbor in for questioning."

Holly closed her eyes and took a deep breath, trying to control her anger. Opening them, she said a curt *thank you* to the officers. Turning on her heel, she walked back to her building with Luke following. "I understand having to do things by the book," she said as she marched up to her door. "But the book is too slow in my opinion."

Speeding back into his apartment, she grabbed her

computer and walked back out into the hall.

Confused, Luke asked, "What are you doing?"

She turned and looked him in the eye. "I meant what I said before, I think we need space to clear our heads."

Having managed to sleep for only a few hours, she spent most of the night tossing and turning, thinking about Kate, her mind in a constant loop of guilt. *It should have been me that was taken, it's my fault that Kate's gone and Luke is probably next* were just some of the thoughts that raced through her mind over and over during the long night. Her gut told her to get away from him, as fast as possible, before something happened to him, too.

Visibly shaken by her statement, he moved fast, positioning himself next to the doorframe while she unlocked it. "Holly, don't be ridiculous."

She snapped her head toward him, anger in her eyes. "You think I'm being *ridiculous* because my best friend is missing and maybe I don't want anything else to happen to someone I—" she stopped for a moment. "—I care about, okay?"

Realizing he chose the wrong words, he stepped back. "I just meant maybe our emotions are crazy right now and you shouldn't be alone."

Looking defeated, Holly opened the door to her apartment. "We've only known each other for a few weeks. I'm not worth all this stress, okay? Just stay away from me for a while."

Stepping over the threshold, Luke shot an arm across the doorframe, blocking access into the apartment. "Don't you think I should be the one to decide if you're worth it?"

Holly hung her head, holding back the tears she

knew were lingering. "Luke, I don't want to see you anymore, okay?"

She heard him suck in a breath, then say in a low, steady voice, "I know you don't mean that."

"You don't know anything about me. I've just been dumped and needed a rebound. I'm sorry to tell you but that's all you were. I should've stopped it sooner when it was clear your feelings were more evolved than mine."

Luke's arm fell to his side, allowing her to pass. "That's not true, and you know it."

Her heart broke, but she kept her guard up and her face emotionless. "It is. Goodbye, Luke."

She shut the door with him still standing there. She fastened the locks, then remembering they could still be picked, took one of the chairs from around the table and wedged it under the doorknob.

She repeated the actions on the back door as well, taking care not to look out the window until she drew the blinds. She didn't want to chance glancing into Luke's kitchen, in case he was in there. Once she felt secure, Holly collapsed onto her couch, bringing her knees to her chest, and let herself finally cry.

He was right of course. Nothing of what she told him was true. She'd developed real feelings for Luke, honest to God feelings that she'd never felt with anyone else. She found herself daydreaming about waking up next to him every morning. She thought about what her parents would say about him, how her brothers would love him, if she would be able to blend in with his family. None of that mattered anymore. She heard Allie's voice in her mind over and over.

Everything will blow up, the King of Swords will lead you to the Tower...

Was this it? Maybe she was the King and blew everything up.

She stood from the couch and opened Kate's door, heeding the advice to stay out of the room. She kept to the door frame as she surveyed the destroyed room. If some psycho had taken her best friend—from a secure, locked apartment—what would happen to Luke?

Although, she thought to herself, *Luke is a big guy who could put up a fight but then...* Holly walked into the room and looked around. *Kate would have put up a fight, too.* She peered at the bed. *She used to take self-defense classes; she definitely would've made a lot more noise than what we heard.*

She walked out and came back with a tissue. If she was going to investigate, she did not want to contaminate the crime scene. She poked around the bed, gingerly lifting and putting the pillows back where they fell and raising the folds of the summer-weight comforter off the corner off the bed. Something odd caught her eye. In the corner, almost falling into the crevice between the mattress and wall, she found a tiny piece of cotton. Using the tissue, she picked it up and studied it. It looked like it had been ripped off a larger piece of the same cotton. It reminded her of the never-ending chain of thin cotton pads manicurists used to take off nail polish.

She tried to remember if Kate had done her nails recently and checked around for bottles of polish bottles or discarded pads and found nothing. She brought the piece closer to her nose and sniffed. She stopped feeling ridiculous when she realized there was something on it, brought it closer to her nose and sniffed again. The scent reminded her of a doctor's office, or bleach.

Placing the tissue on the bed, she looked around the

room for some sort of cleaner, hoping to explain the smell. She opened the closet door and she got on all fours to look under the bed, nothing. So, what was a piece of cotton, broken off from a larger piece, that was covered in some disinfectant doing in Kate's bed? Could the police have left it when they cleaned? Did they even take the time to clean up at crime scenes? Holly shook her head, again feeling silly.

Grabbing her evidence, she went into her own room and sat down at her desk. Opening her laptop, she began to think. The screen blinked to life and her eyes went to the bookmarked bar where the *Murder for Your Thoughts* logo resided. She clicked the button and began to scroll back through old posts. While R.J. mainly wrote about crimes, from time to time they also wrote about topics like tools, means, motives and the psyche of criminals. It took a few minutes to find the article entitled *The Scientific Method: Chemicals of Killers.*

R.J. listed many chemicals telling her readers the names, the uses, and the cases in which they had been used. Her eyes skimmed until she found the word chloroform and stopped to carefully read:

Chloroform: Ah yes, the one and only chloroform. The chemical everyone knows about due to its comedic use in movies and television. It used to be used as an anesthesia back in the olden days (And still today I guess) and was found in lots of medicines just like our other favorite substance, cocaine.

Way back when, H.H. Holmes used it to drug the ladies in his murder hotel. Casey Anthony was thought to have drugged her child with it. Dr. Thomas Cream killed multiple women under the guise of helping them. Chloroform is the drug to rule them all.

Something I always wondered was 'What does chloroform smell like?' So, I did what any normal girl would do and googled it, all the while thinking 'Whatever government organization is looking at my search history today is going to be in for a head scratcher.'

Well after an extensive search and a confirmation from my friends in the medical community, I came to receive this answer: Chloroform can give off an almost sweet smell, some liken it to a disinfectant or association with medical grade cleanliness.

Holly's eyes went wide. *That could be why there wasn't a lot of noise,* she thought. *Kate was drugged.*

Holly smiled, feeling proud of herself for figuring it out but then immediately felt dread when she realized Kate and five other women had been drugged and kidnapped. She grabbed her phone and dialed the non-emergency number for the Chicago police.

After waiting on hold, a surly voice answered the phone. "Lakeview Precinct, what is your issue?"

"Hi, my name is Holly Harrison, I have uh…an ongoing investigation? Can you please connect me with either Officer Martinez or Shane?" The officer on the other side of the phone sighed, and she envisioned him rolling his eyes at the receiver. "Hold on."

She was placed back on hold. Holly looked at the phone before putting it back to her ear; clearly someone hated phone duty. After another moment, a familiar voice answered on the other end. "Martinez."

"Hi, Officer, um this is Holly Harrison. You've been to my house a few times? Er, uh, because my neighbor is a bad guy?" Holly smacked her palm to her forehead cursing herself for being so awkward on the phone. She literally did this for a living, why couldn't she keep it together? To her surprise, the sound of a low chuckle rang through her cell phone.

"Yes, Holly, I know who you are. Trust me, you are hard to forget."

She felt herself blush. "Yes, well, um, I know you guys told me not to, but I went into Kate's room. Before you yell at me, I didn't touch anything directly, I used a tissue and I didn't disturb anything, but I figured it would be a good idea if I looked around since I live here and know Kate and what goes where in her room so I thought maybe I could just see if anything looked super fishy?"

Again, her blabbering was met with chuckling. "Miss Harrison, you live there so your DNA is all over everything, so contamination wasn't an issue. However, you really should not have gone in there—"

Before he could finish his admonishment, Holly cut him off. "I found something."

There was a pause before he asked in a slow, curious manner. "What did you find?"

She filled him in about the cotton, the smell, and how in her opinion it had to be chloroform. After she was done, there was a pause on the other end of the line, he was thinking everything over. "Okay. Sit tight. I'm on my way."

She was taken aback at his conclusion. "I mean, shouldn't I just give it to the officers outside?"

"The shift is almost up and there is going to be a change anyways, I'll be there soon." With that, he hung up and Holly felt hopeful, she might finally be getting answers.

Chapter Twenty

Officer Martinez arrived at five o'clock with a loud rap on Holly's door. When she opened it to let him in, she saw Luke open his door at the same time, looking alert. "Is everything all right? What is he doing here?" He ignored the uniformed man, speaking directly to her.

Holding her chin high she spoke nonchalantly. "Don't worry about it." She then turned toward Martinez. "Please come in."

Luke started to say, "Holly, wait—" but was cut off as she closed the door on him.

Officer Martinez showed a look of confusion. "Lovers' quarrel?"

She shook her head. "Just a tiff between neighbors."

He raised his eyebrows but said nothing as she quickly walked past him into her bedroom. "The cotton is in here."

She grabbed it off her desk and turned only to see he followed her into the bedroom, standing with his hands tucked into his vest. When he'd stood beside his partner, he'd looked shorter. Here, in her room, and all alone, he seemed to take up the whole space.

She inhaled a waft of his cologne as he moved closer to her outstretched hand. Martinez took the tissue, opened it, and studied it closely. Satisfied with what he saw, he took out a small plastic baggie placing both the tissue and the piece of cotton inside.

"Can you show me where in her room you found it?"

Nodding, she made to move past him, her chest brushed against his torso as she passed in the small space. Again, she caught a whiff of cologne and looked up to meet his kind smile. She averted her gaze and led the way to Kate's room. Stopping at her roommate's bedside, she motioned to the corner in which she found the cotton.

He moved next to the mattress and while he bent down to inspect the area, she took the time to inspect him. He was a lot more muscular than she realized, filling out his black, short sleeved uniform. He reached across the bed, and Holly noticed the bottom of a tattoo on his upper bicep. Her eyes wandered up to his dark hair, cut close on the sides but a bit longer on top. She could not deny he was a good-looking guy.

Straightening up, he looked around the rest of the room. "Did you find anything else in here that didn't seem normal?"

"I looked for something to explain the cotton, but I'll give it a quick sweep now."

He stepped back as she moved past and started to investigate the desk. "So, you and your neighbor are just friends?"

She paused and looked behind her at the man as he dug through Kate's bedside table. She responded as she turned back to her task. "Kind of? I don't really know; I've had a few other things on my mind."

"Of course," he said in a hurried manner. "I just meant, you were staying in his apartment and you two seemed a little, I don't know, glued at the hip."

She sighed as she moved on, looking at the area around Kate's desk. "We were, it's just, cooling off for the moment, I guess. Okay I don't see anything funky over here. You?"

Officer Martinez closed the drawer and looked over. "Nothing for me either but it was worth a shot, considering we already missed something the first time."

"So, what happens now?" she asked as they walked out into the living room.

He turned, resting his hands inside his vest. "I'll take this cotton back and have the lab run tests. If there is chloroform, we'll know how he's getting the girls out without a sound." Rifling through his pocket, he produced a card. "This has my direct line on it. I want you to have it in case anything else happens, that way you don't have to be put on hold. I already have your number so when I get results, I'll call you."

"Thanks, Officer."

"You can call me Ben."

Fidgeting with the card, Holly felt herself flush. "Thank you, Officer Ben." That earned her a laugh, and she felt herself relax a bit.

He walked toward the door and threw parting words over his shoulder. "I'll be on watch tonight so don't worry about being in here alone."

"Ben, wait." His name sounded strange on her tongue, but she powered on. "Would you be able to walk around the building a few times? I've got all these locks and I'm wedging a chair under the knob but I'm...I'm worried it's not enough."

Holly could feel tears starting to form, and she quickly looked away so he wouldn't see. His feet shuffled and his hand thrust in front of her, holding a tissue. She took it, head still down, and dabbed at her eyes. When she was sure she had stopped the tears, she looked up into his kind gaze.

"I'll make sure to circle the building, check the front and back door." His voice had taken on a gentler tone, a contrast to the professional way she was used to. "You will be able to sleep uninterrupted tonight, okay?"

"I'll sleep after you bring him in for questioning."

He smiled and walked back to the door. "I think it'll be soon. Good night, Holly." He opened the door and walked out into the hall with her trailing behind.

"Good night, Ben." She closed and locked the door behind him and went back to her bedroom getting ready to turn in, thinking about everything that had happened that day.

Feeling flattered at the attention from Ben, she knew if circumstances were different, she might have been interested in pursuing him. But she met Luke first. She had fallen for him, even though she had let him go. When all of this was over, she would go knock on his door, explain everything, and hopefully he would give her another chance, but for now she had to stay firm in her stance. No more people would get hurt on her behalf.

Later as she drifted off to sleep, her head filled with images of Luke wearing a police uniform. Tight shirt, putting her in hand cuffs...she awoke with a start and groaned. It was not going to be a restful night after all.

****

Luke woke that morning in a foul mood. The night before he was tossing and turning, picturing Officer Martinez and Holly together, alone, in her apartment. He kicked his sheets into a ball around his feet in frustration as he lay there, staring at the ceiling.

Or is it Ben? They're on a first name basis now.

What happened that Holly had felt the need to call

186

Ben? He turned onto his stomach and grabbed his phone. He scrolled through to see if there were any new texts or calls from her. Nothing.

He slammed his phone down on the nightstand and headed to the bathroom to take a shower. Yanking the shower handle to hot, he continued to think about Holly and what she said to him the night before. He knew she said all of that to…protect him? Which didn't seem to make sense since she was clearly the target, not him, and she needed someone with her, to watch her back. Is this why she had called Officer Martinez? Because she trusted him more than Luke? He shook that thought out of his head, remembering their time at the lake house. The connection they both felt could not be faked. The electricity that sparked between them in the lake, in the bedroom…

He dried off, dressed, and went to his room to grab his laptop. He heard a knock coming from the hallway and went to the front door to look out the peephole.

Officer Martinez stood in front of Holly's door, two cups of coffee in his hand. Holly answered the door wearing her oversized shirt and tiny shorts, her hair was wild and messy around her shoulders. Their conversation was muffled through the door, but he could read their body language. *Ben* had bought a coffee for her, she smiled and accepted it, and…she was inviting him into her apartment? Again?

He watched through the peephole as she closed the door and he slammed his fist against the wall. He went and sat on the couch, dropping his head in his hands. Maybe he needed to accept that this was, in fact, what she wanted. Maybe he shouldn't try to fight for her. Not knowing how long he sat like that, he was suddenly woken from his trance by a knock at his door.

Confused, he opened it to see Officer Martinez on the other side, looking a bit out of place and awkward. "Hello, Mr. Morris, may I come in?"

Luke nodded stiffly, moving aside as Martinez walked past him into the living room. "Thanks for letting me in. I wanted to give you an update on the case since you've been involved from the start and it seems like now, uh, you might not be totally in the loop anymore?"

He trailed off and Luke raised an eyebrow but stayed silent as he crossed his arms and moved closer to the officer. Martinez was tall but he was taller and the closer he got, the more the officer had to tilt his head up to look at him. It was petty but, at the moment, he didn't care.

Unfazed, Martinez continued speaking. "I mean, it seems like you and Holly are uh, no longer together?"

Luke scowled. "She thinks she's protecting me by keeping her distance from me. I'm going to respect her wishes to not bother her now, but we are going to get back together as soon as you guys arrest our neighbor."

Officer Martinez's lips quirked up. "That's exactly why I'm here. Holly found something last night, and we had it tested. Seems there was chloroform used in the kidnapping, and we now have enough evidence to ask this Phil person in for questioning."

His arms dropped and the scowl shifted to a look of awe. "That's incredible."

"Slow down, it's good but only questioning for now. I'm hoping the tests come back for the shirt while we have him there, but I can't guarantee anything."

Luke nodded but couldn't help getting his hopes up at the thought of this being over and he and Holly celebrating together. Martinez smirked and headed back toward the door. "I'll continue to let you know any updates, okay?"

"Yes, thank you, Officer."

Luke watched him walk out of the building. He waited a beat before he crossed the hall and knocked on Holly's door, careful to avoid the peephole in case she didn't want to open the door for him.

She answered the door with the coffee cup in her hand and a smile which fell when she saw him. Luke chose to ignore that nonverbal punch to the gut. "I just got the news from Martinez. Phil is being taken in."

"Yeah, Ben told me, too."

"Ben?"

A blush spread over her cheeks as she quickly backtracked. "He told me to call him by his first name last night. I called him in because I found something in Kate's room that I thought could help and, since we keep having to call him, he just thought…" She looked down at her feet as she let her sentence hang there.

He dreaded what could be the end to her unfinished sentence but became distracted by the sight of a chair next to the door. "Why is that there?"

"Oh, I'm using it to prop under the doorknob, you know, extra protection."

Luke ran a frustrated hand through his hair. "Jeez, Hol. Just come over and stay with me. I would feel a lot better if—"

She put her hand on his chest. "Stop, please. Did you even listen to me last night? I need to be here, stay here in my own apartment, okay?"

He straightened as she let her hand fall to her side. "Oh, I listened. Listened to you tell lies to make you feel like you're keeping me safe. I understand that you feel like Kate was your fault, but it wasn't."

"Yes, it was. Of course, it was my fault. It should've been me; I should've been kidnapped since I'm the one that keeps sticking my nose in someone else's business. Excuse me if I don't want something to happen to you."

She looked on the verge of crying. Luke made a move to embrace her, but she stepped back out of reach. "Don't. Please, just don't."

Feeling helpless, he dropped his arms and took a step back. "I'm not going to stop because I know what we have is real. I'm right here, and I'm not going anywhere. I'm going to sit on the back porch and do work if you change your mind."

Without looking at him or saying another word, she closed the door on him for the second time in two days. He stood out there for a moment, gathering his thoughts. Back in his apartment, he grabbed his computer and went to the back porch to begin work. He looked into the now empty apartment on the second floor and felt uneasy. Even though Phil had now been brought in to be questioned by the police, he had a bad feeling that this ordeal was not over.

Every so often he found himself looking up to see if Holly's blinds were still closed, which they were. Around lunch time he saw a flurry of movement and looked up, the blinds moved as if they had just been opened and shut. He smiled knowing he was right, and that she still cared.

Chapter Twenty-One

As the day passed, Holly estimated that she peeked out her back window overlooking the porch at least twenty times. She was frustrated with herself for looking so often. Why did she even care that he was out there? She couldn't help but look out the window at the beautiful man out there every time she went into the kitchen. It was just a never-ending circle.

As night fell, Holly turned on the nine o' clock news, hoping to see Phil actually being arrested. Segment after segment passed and nothing pertaining to him, or the missing ladies, aired. Disappointed, she turned off the TV and made her way to her room. She felt sad, alone, exhausted, and wanted to sleep for the next week. As she got into bed and tried not to cry, again, her cell phone rang, and she saw it was Officer Martinez.

"Ben?"

"Holly, listen. He's gone."

"Wait what? Who is gone?"

"Your neighbor is gone, and it's not good." There was a shuffling on the other end of the line before he spoke again. "We questioned him, brought up the shirt, but he did not provide us with DNA. Lucky for us he accepted the coffee we offered so we scooped that cup up when he wasn't looking, but then during the break in questioning, he somehow managed to disappear."

Exhaustion vanished as her anxiety rose. "What do

you mean, *disappear*?"

"We don't understand it, but he just got up and left, and somehow none of us saw it. So, whatever you do, stay inside with all the doors locked. Do you understand?"

Holly gripped the phone tighter. "Have you checked the storage locker?"

"You didn't hear this from me, but no, not yet. I'm still waiting on a warrant."

Holly quickly replied, "But what if Kate is there? What if—"

He cut her off. "Like I said before, stay inside and let us handle this. I can't go barging in, but I will do everything I can as quickly as I can." His tone softened before he continued. "You'll be safe inside."

"Okay." Her voice came out much softer than she intended.

"I'll let you know more when I know more."

"Thanks." She ended the call.

Now, Holly felt terrified and vulnerable in what she once considered the safety of her bed. A dangerous man was on the loose, one that she helped make a prime suspect. She got out of bed, ready to further barricade herself in when she stopped. *He wouldn't come here, especially if the cops are still parked out front.*

She raced to her window and peeked through the blinds to see the now familiar sight of a cop car parked down the block. *If he isn't coming here, that means he wouldn't go home, so where else would he go?*

While thinking of the possibilities, she quickly changed from her pajamas into capri-length leggings and a loose T-shirt, there was no way she could just stay in and go to bed now.

The only idea that kept coming to mind was that Phil would run to his storage unit. Why would he go there rather than run out of the city? She did not know, but her gut told her the answers hid behind that large, ugly, orange door. Her breath was coming fast, and her heart was beating hard in her chest as the plan further formed in her mind. She jammed her feet into her sneakers and left her apartment, pausing before she got to the stairs that led outside. She turned and knocked on Luke's door, realizing that her hands were shaking.

He answered quickly, opening the door to reveal himself in what Holly had come to think of as his nighttime uniform— shirtless with basketball shorts. He looked serious as he glanced over Holly's outfit. "What's wrong, where are you going?"

Holly stood, her hands trembled, and her voice felt fragile. "Phil's escaped."

He moved toward her but stopped in his tracks. Holly felt lightheaded and swayed slightly, the shock of it all finally settling in. He snapped out of whatever internal debate he was having and moved, placing a hand to the small of her back and slowly led her inside. "You need to sit down. I'm going to get you a glass of water."

Parking her safely on the couch, Luke went to the kitchen while Holly stared off into space. Until then, she hadn't said it out loud, and the shock of it and what she was planning to do sucked all of the adrenaline from her body. It left her feeling like she was floating, unable to anchor to the ground.

Luke came back into the room, sitting next to her on the couch, and urged her to drink the contents of the glass he pressed into her hand. After a few small sips, Holly felt a bit more awake, alert.

He waited until he made sure she would not faint before he asked his question. "What do you mean Phil has escaped?"

Holly kept her gaze on the glass in her hands as she spoke low and fast, the words pouring out of her mouth. "Ben called and said while they took a break from questions, he somehow slipped out of the building. I'm sure he's so used to being a wallflower it just came easy to him. He told me all of this then said to stay inside until they find Phil."

Luke gave her a small smile. "So, you decided to come here?"

"No." She looked at him straight on. "I decided to go find him." Luke's brow furrowed in confusion as she continued. "He isn't going to come here or go back to his own house, not with the police parked right out front."

"Whoa, Holly, slow down, you don't know that. He was able to tape a note to your door without them seeing, I wouldn't put it past him to be a complete psycho and go for the gold."

"No, not when he's just slipped out of their grasp. I think he's going to go to his storage unit and finish…I don't know, finish what he started, I guess. I want to go to the unit and open it and see what's in there and—" She took a deep breath. "I want you to come with me."

Luke said nothing but continued to stare at her. Holly looked into his eyes, those green, almost hypnotic eyes, silently pleading for him to go with her. When he finally spoke, his voice came out like gravel. "I understand why you want to go, and part of me is tempted too, but this situation is even more dangerous now. Officer Martinez will have gotten the word out, and I'm sure a lot of police are looking for him right now. I think the smart thing to do would be to stay put for the time being."

She stood up quickly, spilling water on the floor. Frustrated, she held back the tears that threatened to fall. She felt at a loss at what to do but knew she couldn't just sit waiting for news.

Luke stood, closing the space between their bodies, and put his forehead to hers. "Please, just stay here with me, where it's safe."

Closing her eyes, she felt the tears roll down her face. "You don't understand. What if Kate is in there? I can't—" She broke off as her voice cracked, not trusting herself to continue.

"If we don't hear anything by the morning, I'll go with you. I can't...I can't have anything happen to you. It would kill me."

She felt defeated as she gave the tiniest nod in surrender and Luke's body relaxed. He lifted his head and wrapped his arms around her, his hand snaking up the back of her neck to tangle in her hair and held her against him.

She buried her face in his chest, allowing herself to relax against his body and cry. She tried to speak but all that came out was the word "Kate" followed by another sob. Luke scooped her up, and Holly wrapped her arms around his neck.

He whispered soothing sentiments in her ear as he carried her to his bedroom. When he began to pull his arms away after placing her on the bed but stopped when Holly tightened her hold around his neck. "No."

Luke scooted her farther onto the mattress and laid himself down next to her, their faces inches apart. The intimacy of the moment overwhelmed Holly. She continued to cry as Luke brushed the hair out of her eyes.

His fingers lingered and wiped away a tear from her cheek. "I'm so sorry, love."

She put her hands on either side of his face. "No, I'm sorry. I'm sorry for everything."

She closed the space between them and covered his mouth with hers. She inhaled his scent, felt the prickle of his stubble on her cheek, as her fingers drifted up to entwine in his hair. Her thin T-shirt was all that separated her from his bare chest, she ran her free hand down his pecs, raking her nails slowly back up. Her hand drifted lower and lower and, as her hips pressed against his, she felt him bulging against his nylon shorts. She pulled back to catch her breath, and Luke put his hands on her shoulders, stopping her as she reached to pull off her shirt.

"Holly I…I feel like this isn't a good idea right now. I mean, you're worked up and so am I and it's really crazy right now." His eyes searched hers, but all she wanted was to not be reminded of everything happening at the moment. She pushed off him and sat up, feeling rejected and vulnerable. He put a hand on her back, but she shook it off.

She stood up and wiped the wetness from her face. "Sorry for that."

She started to walk out of the room, but Luke leapt up from the bed and blocked her path to the door. "Whoa, where are you going?"

She looked up at him. "Away from here."

"I thought we just decided on you staying the night. Please, it's not that I don't want this, don't want you… I just, I don't want you to regret something." He scratched the back of his head awkwardly.

She softened slightly and discreetly checked the time on her phone. It was ten o'clock, and her anxiety heightened. She needed to do something. "I have all this energy, and I don't want to think about anything that's happening, I need a distraction, I need to do something."

Her hands could not stop fidgeting as she looked everywhere except at Luke, she did not need to see his pity. He was silent for what seemed like minutes, but was probably only seconds, until she felt his hand softly cup her face. He gently turned her head to face him.

"We can always lift some weights if you want to burn off energy." Despite all the fear, anger, and anxiety, Holly laughed at the dumb joke and straight-faced delivery. Her shoulders started to release some of the tension as Luke continued. "I know this sucks, but I'm only trying to help."

She sighed heavily. "Okay." She walked back to the bed and got in, leaving Luke standing there, perplexed. She offered, "Let's watch something?" He got into bed, attempting to shift close to her, but Holly offered a hand instead. After a moment of hesitation, he reached over interlacing their fingers.

For the next half hour, the two sat in silence while keeping their eyes on the television which had been switched to a random 90's sitcom. Holly stayed as still as possible, taking care to not shift and make the mattress creak, and soon enough she heard Luke's breath even out. Risking a glance to her left confirmed he had fallen asleep. Very slowly she began to inch off the bed until the only thing left connecting her was their entwined hands. She hesitated, part of her wanted to stay here, in the safety of his room. Then an image of Kate popped into her mind reminding herself what she needed to do.

Un-lacing their fingers, she placed his hand as gently as possible back onto the mattress and looked back at his unconscious form. She was reminded of when she had seen him sleeping at the lake house, how she thought he looked like an angel. His head was tilted so that his jawbone angled upward, the hairs along it shining with the light of the television. Holly thought about him waking to see her gone and felt her stomach drop. She quietly left the room, grabbing a pen and a stack of sticky notes and wrote, *I had to go see for myself, I'm sorry.*

After a moment she added, *I love you.*

She chickened out saying it out loud to him already and if something were to happen to her tonight, well at least he would know how she had felt all along.

She placed the note on the pillow she had been lying against and grabbed one of his sweatshirts from the ground. She inhaled the scent of his cologne on the fabric before pulling it over her head, took one last look at the man she loved, and quietly left through the front door.

Chapter Twenty-Two

Maybe this wasn't such a good idea.

She sped down the main road to the storage building. With every step she took, her self-doubt grew more, but then Kate's face would pop into her mind. *She'd do the same for me.*

That thought would make her walk faster. The time on her phone read ten forty-five. Businesses had already been closed for at least an hour, and there were very few people out on the street. Holly realized this was the first time in a long time that she was by herself while it was dark outside. It made her uneasy that the buzz of the city, of diners leaving restaurants, of cars zooming by, were not ringing out across the neighborhood. She crossed her arms and shivered as the wind blew. Looking over her shoulder, she scanned the mostly empty street. She thought the storage unit was a lot closer, but maybe that is because she had Luke with her then.

Luke.

Her mind filled with guilt, picturing him waking up and her not being there. He would be angry and hurt. Her original plan was to go look at the storage unit and if she did not find anything, race back and be in bed before he noticed. If she found something, hopefully Kate, everyone would be too happy to be mad at her, so it was really a win-win in her mind.

Crash.

She came to a stop and watched as a rat ran out of the alleyway. She let out a sigh of relief and then a humorless chuckle; if she was relieved to see a rodent, she had to reprioritize her life. Resuming her walk, she looked up and realized she was almost to her destination. The lit sign of the storage unit flickered, and she did a double take, realizing she did not notice the name of the storage company.

Tower Units.

Once again, she heard Allie's voice in her head reminding her, she would get clarity when the King led her to the Tower. She walked on and made a mental note to never doubt her friend again because she was totally a real witch.

As she drew nearer the building, she checked the large pocket of her borrowed sweatshirt. After leaving Luke's apartment, she had run back to hers and quickly grabbed a few bobby pins, a safety pin, tweezers, and a small pair of cuticle scissors from a manicure bag. Since she did not have actual lock picking tools, she figured she would grab anything that was a small, pointy object and try her luck picking the lock to the unit.

She approached the door and looked around, not a soul was out on the street but her. Praying that a higher power was on her side, she pulled on the handle to the door and, just like last time, it swung open with no issue. Cautiously, she walked inside and passed the still empty desk to peer through the small window. Checking to see if anyone was in the hallway containing the lockers, she silently turned the handle and opened the door. Holly stopped only to hear if there were any footsteps. Dead silence.

At the end of the gray hallway, she came to a halt at

the orange door that Phil once stood in front of. Taking one more look around and to make sure no one was coming, she knelt and got her 'tools' out of her pocket.

Holly tugged on the lock, hoping her luck would work a second time and, to her dismay, it did not budge. She took out a bobby pin first and began wiggling it around in the keyhole. After a few attempts she sighed and took out her phone and found an online video on how to pick a lock.

Five excruciatingly long minutes later, she was about to give up when she felt a click. Her heart stopped and she held her breath. This was the plan, to open the lock, look in the unit, and go home, but she had not really believed it was going to come to fruition until now. Slowly starting to let herself breathe again and steadying her shaking hands, she carefully unhooked the lock and paused.

Holly had never broken a law, except for when she broke into Phil's apartment, and it had just dawned on her that this was definitely illegal. Looking around again, she felt assured at seeing no one. She lifted the door as she stood up and gasped.

She expected to see a storage unit littered with nefarious tools and Kate tied up or something along those lines, but laid out before her was a confusingly large space, almost completely dark save for one small dim lightbulb that flickered in the back, right-hand corner. It had to be four or five separate units, the walls removed to create the almost cavernous room before her.

Slowly, she crept into the space, running her hands along the walls trying to feel for some sort of light switch. Her fingers located it and flipped it up, casting light on the rest of the area. In the middle of the room sat a large metal table with two chairs on either side. Handcuffs hung off the arms of one of the chairs. Horrified, Holly started slowly walking along the wall to her right, taking everything in.

Starting clockwise around the room she saw there was a small desk with some papers scattered on the surface, a filing cabinet, and a small upright piano all lined up to her left. The wall to her right held no furniture, but instead had photos taped on every inch of surface available. Photos taken of women, clearly without their knowledge, with circles around their faces. As she walked, the realization dawned that these were the girls who had been taken. She stopped in her tracks as she came to the last picture. It was a photo of her, taken through a window, capturing her sitting at her desk. Holly felt sick to her stomach at the thought of Phil watching her. Telling herself to keep moving, she looked up and was met with a wall of black fabric. What she thought was the back of the room was actually just a curtain, cutting the space in half. She took a deep breath and gently pulled the curtain back.

Large cages, big enough to fit a giant dog, lined the back wall, each one spaced two to four feet from the next one. Two bowls sat beside each cage, one filled with water and the other empty, probably used for food. Each one was occupied by a small, unmoving mass covered with a blanket. Holly rushed to the one closest to her and tried to open it. There was another padlock, older than the one on the storage room door, keeping the cage shut, but Holly did not have the patience to try and pick another one. Instead, she looked around for something heavy and decided to use the metal food bowl. Using all her strength, she smashed the bowl down and popped the lock off on her third try. Flinging the door open, she grabbed and pulled the blanket off revealing her unconscious friend. Tears immediately sprang to her eyes as she gently tried to shake her awake.

"Oh my God, Kate. Please wake up, please, please, please."

Her hands flew to Kate's neck as she searched for a pulse. After what felt like an eternity, she found the faint beat and quickly said a prayer of thanks to every religious idol she could think of.

"Can you hear me?"

She patted Kate's cheek until her eyes started fluttering. Relieved that there was some sort of response, she grabbed Kate's legs and dragged her as gently as possible out of the cage. Propping her up into a sitting position, she knelt down next to her, studying her face, looking for any signs of harm, finding neither bruises nor cuts. There was nothing to suggest that she was physically hurt.

Her eyes moved down to Kate's hands, her knuckles were riddled with tiny scrapes and some of her nails were broken. Holly smiled to herself; she knew she was a fighter. Lifting the sleeve of her T-shirt, she found what she was looking for: a small, red puncture mark was visible against the pink skin. Anger bubbled as she pulled the sleeve back down and sat back on her heels. He drugged all these women.

She looked to her left; now to open the other cages. She looked back at the food bowl she had just used; it was totally bent and would not be of use. She tried anyways, banging the bowl against the lock of the next cage but was met with resistance. Holly turned to her roommate, putting a hand to her barely conscious

203

friend's cheek. "I'll be right back. Stay with me, Kate, I know you're in there."

She scrambled back around the curtain; eyes trained to the floor looking for something heavy. She stopped in her tracks as the tinkling of piano keys began to sound. Trembling, she looked up to see Phil sitting at the piano, playing the familiar sad, slow tune she heard him play a million times before.

He turned his head without stopping his fingers. "Oh, hi neighbor."

He turned back and played the next few notes with a flourish. Holly looked at the door, thinking about making a run for it, and saw that it was shut.

"You know I play this for you right? The first time I played it, you were sitting outside, and you looked up from your computer and smiled. I enjoyed making you smile, so I made sure to play it only when you were sitting outside."

Holly immediately took stock of what was around her, looking for anything that could be used as a weapon. Maybe if she threw herself against the wall and pulled off his creepy collage he would be so upset and distracted that she could...

What—overpower him? Holly was not a waif, but Phil kidnapped and dragged all these girls here without being seen. He probably had super psycho strength that would easily overpower her. What do they do in the movies? Keep them talking.

"How did you escape the police?" She slowly started to bring her right hand, currently loose at her side, around to her back pocket which contained her phone. If she could subtly dial 911, she could get all the girls out safely.

Phil closed the lid of the piano and stood, pivoting to face her. His stance reminded Holly of a gunslinger, hands out to his sides, ready for anything. Craziness radiated from his eyes while his thin lips were glued in a smile. The disheveled thin blond hair—he had clearly run here— stuck out at all angles in random places. He wore a loose white T-shirt that accentuated the paleness of his skin, dark jeans, and a pair of work boots.

"It's easy to just walk out of places when no one notices you. I've always been pretty good at blending in, not being seen. Except for you, you seem to see me." His features softened, looking at her like he was almost touched. Holly tried to hide her revulsion.

"You see me and take notice of me. I've been waiting to find the one who would see me just like I see them." He gestured to the wall of photos, his features contorting to that of disgust. "I thought they saw me, I felt like they saw me, but they were all lying. Lying whores, the lot of them, but you"—he turned back to Holly, his expression lightening again—"you're different."

"So that's why you broke in and kidnapped women against their will? Because you thought they were insane like you? Hate to break it to you, but I'm just like them." Her hand reached her pocket, and she inched the phone out. Now to figure out how to dial a number on a touchscreen while not looking. She took a slow step to her right, maybe if she stood by the slab or the desk, she could hide her hand. Phil had moved to the wall of photos and touched a few, still maintaining eye contact with her. Every time he stepped, so did she, keeping them on opposite sides of an invisible circle.

"You're nothing like them, you're different. You are

beautiful, kind, caring, you're the perfect one for me. I'll forgive you for seeing the neighbor, you didn't know we were supposed to be together, but you're here alone tonight so it must mean you've come to your senses. I forgave you for following me to my workspace." He raised his hands, gesturing to the room they occupied.

Curiosity got the better of her as she continued with questioning. "Why were you mad that night? We saw you yelling into the phone."

He smiled. "Someone reported hearing sounds. I wasn't happy that my girls were making noises, so I had to fix their dosage, keep them sleeping."

He tilted his head toward her. "You know I forgave you again for coming into my room." She stopped walking, and his smile widened. "Oh, yes, I knew about that. I smelled your shampoo all over my room."

Holly silently cursed her choices in fragrant hair care products.

Phil continued. "I was mad at first, so mad, but then I thought about you, in my room, touching my things and it got me...excited." Holly's eyes widened in fear. "Even thinking about it now..." He closed his eyes and breathed in, giving her a chance to take a large step so the metal slab hid the bottom half of her body. She hazarded a glance down, unlocking her phone, and looked back up. Phil opened his eyes and turned his body toward her, to her disgust he was getting visibly aroused, she needed to shut this guy down, now.

She moved against the table and heard the tiniest metallic clang ring from the sweatshirt pocket. She forgot that she had tweezers and cuticle scissors. Feeling emboldened, she decided to keep him talking as she moved her thumb around, hurriedly trying to dial 911.

"So, when you realized these girls, uh, weren't like me, you just, kept them here?"

He nodded, taking a step closer toward her. She was unable to move or else she would show her phone. "And you didn't think I wouldn't be jealous of all these girls?"

He stopped in his tracks, his smile gone. Panic painted his face. "I...I made you jealous?"

"Yep, you sure did. And mad. You took my friend instead of me. How do you think that makes me feel?"

She finally dialed, why wasn't the call going through? In the moment her eyes looked down, Phil lunged at her, knocking her off balance and sending them both tumbling to the ground. Her phone skittered out of her grasp as she pushed at him and rolled away only to have him grab hold of her ankles.

"Didn't you know there's no cell phone service in here? That's the great thing about multiple layers of concrete." She tried to kick free, but he held on tighter confirming her earlier thoughts about that psycho strength. He pulled her toward him, and she screamed out for help but was only met with a chuckle from Phil.

Thinking fast, Holly reached into her pocket and grabbed the tiny but sharp pair of cuticle scissors. Ripping them out of her pocket, she jabbed them with all her might into the hand restraining her. He immediately screamed in pain and let go as she scrambled up and out of his grasp to the other side of the slab.

"Stay the fuck away from me," she yelled, brandishing the tiny scissors.

He jumped up, clutching his bleeding hand. "You'll pay for that."

He lunged over the table, but she jumped back, out of his range. "You should just give up now, the cops must be looking for you. And I've told them about this place. It's only a matter of time until they find you."

He made it over the table and was moving like a predator stalking its prey, forcing Holly to stumble blindly toward the wall. She moved to her right until she was met with another wall; he literally had her cornered.

He moved closer, grabbed the wrist of the hand holding the scissors, and yanked them out of her grasp, throwing them behind him. She attempted to punch him, but he caught her fist, pulling it toward him. "Don't worry, I won't hurt you like you hurt me."

He planted a kiss on the inside of her wrist, and she gagged. Luke's beautiful face popped into her head; with it brought a surge of adrenaline. She tried to yank her arm out of Phil's grasp, but he held on tighter. She felt tears prickle her eyes at the pain. She was supposed to save the day, not become another victim written about in a blog.

With one last ditch effort, she brought her knee up, making contact with his groin. He stumbled, loosening his hold on her, which was all she needed. Holly pushed him with all her might, and he fell, bent over in pain and breathing hard.

"You bitch."

Without looking back, Holly ran to the orange door. She lifted it as far as waist height when she felt another body crashing into hers from behind, slamming her head and pinning her against the door. Her vision blurred as she shot out an elbow, hitting Phil right in the nose with a sickening crunch. The two fell, and he landed on top of her, crushing the air out of her lungs and most likely, Holly thought, breaking a rib. Phil moaned in pain as she pushed him off and rolled away. Her fingertips confirmed that blood ran down her face, the face plant into the door left a gash on her forehead. She looked up and saw something shiny a few feet away: the cuticle scissors.

She struggled to crawl, which was no easy feat when her chest felt like it was on fire with every breath she took. Her arm stretched out and gripped the scissors hard in her palm. She looked back at Phil still clutching his face, blood now pouring out between his hands. She hefted herself up to her knees and shuffled back over to him, scissors in hand. Slightly dizzy and now with blood running into her eye, she held the scissors high over her head and brought them down into the largest part of him she could make out, his thigh. The scissors sank in, and Phil screamed with pain, clutching his leg.

She dragged herself away and toward the garage door when suddenly she made out a pair of feet on the other side. Before she could see the owner of the pair of feet, Phil's hand grabbed her ankle, yanking her back. Her knees came out from under her, her body slamming into the floor, screaming in pain as her chest crashed into the concrete. The sound of the garage door fully opening caused both her and Phil to turn their heads. There stood Luke, the light from the hallway framed his body, making him look like he was her guardian angel.

Phil quickly let go of Holly's ankle as Luke ran into the unit. He began to shuffle backward clutching his leg with one hand, still shouting in pain as he attempted to move away. Luke, dropping to his knees, grabbed Holly's shoulders, and hoisted her up to a kneeling position.

"Are you okay? What did he do to you?"

She attempted to stand up, and he helped her up to

lean against the wall. Feeling very woozy now that all the adrenaline was leaving her body, she answered in a hoarse voice. "I'm okay, I hurt him. Kate's here." She lifted her arm, and his gaze followed her finger to land on the yelling Phil. Luke's face changed from one of concern to one of pure rage.

Without a moment of hesitation, he closed the space between him and Phil, grabbed him by the shirt, and lifted him up. "You will never touch her again."

There was a loud crack as Luke's fist connected with Phil's face. If his nose wasn't broken before, it definitely was now. Phil sagged down, clearly dazed, but he kept his hold on him and hit him again. Then a third time.

"Luke, stop."

She started to slide down the wall she was leaning against, realizing that her voice came out quieter than intended. It was proving hard for her to take deep breaths without a sharp pain. Now sitting on the floor, she straightened her back against the wall and tried again.

Forcing herself to speak louder, and wincing through the pain, she said, "Luke. Please, you're going to kill him."

This time her voice hit his ears and Luke looked over his shoulder and loosened his hold on Phil. He rushed to her side and propped her up with concern in his eyes as Holly grimaced at the movement.

She looked up at him and smiled, her head throbbing. "He's not worth going to jail for."

He swallowed hard. A mixture of emotions crossed his face, and he struggled to keep his voice steady. "I beg to differ, anyone who lays a finger on you..." He trailed off as he brushed a fallen piece of hair out of her eyes.

"Told you I wouldn't leave you out, I wrote you a

note." She wheezed. Something dripped onto her hand and looking down at her fingers, she realized she was crying.

His eyes filled with tears as he cradled her with his arms and shifted her weight off the wall and onto him. He slid them down to the floor, cradling her in his arms.

"You did."

"All the girls are here. Kate's here. He kept them in cages." Her voice cracked, and he held her closer. "Go make sure they're all right?"

He shook his head. "The police are almost here, they can attend to the girls. I'm not letting you go. Not again."

"I'm fine—"

"You're crazy if you think I'm going to leave your side." A tear escaped his eye, rolling down his cheek.

A flurry of activity arose behind Holly as multiple officers ran in, brandishing guns.

"He's over there, and so are all the girls," Luke called over his shoulder.

As Holly's head began to bob, his attention snapped back to her. He cupped her head. "Stay awake, love, the ambulance is almost here."

She smiled and mumbled, "You have the most beautiful green eyes."

She promptly passed out, letting herself settle into unconsciousness.

Chapter Twenty-Three

Luke broke a few bones and received a few cuts on his hand from punching Phil. He sat on the hospital bed getting his knuckles bandaged and his fingers set and put into casts. All the while, trying to get a glimpse of Holly though the hospital curtains.

To his relief, she woke up in the ambulance on the way to the hospital. She had a serious concussion and a gash on her forehead, a broken rib, and a plethora of scrapes and bruises. Now placed in the room opposite Luke, she was getting cleaned up by the nurses.

As soon as the last brace was placed on his finger, he rushed to the room containing Holly. Slowly, he opened the door and saw her sitting up in bed with her right eye swollen and bruised. As soon as her eyes found his, she smiled. The nurse bandaging her turned and started to ask him to leave when Holly stopped her. "Please let him stay?"

The nurse raised a skeptical eyebrow. "All right, but only because I'm about done here." She got up and left the room, and Luke sat down next to her on the side of her bed.

"How are you feeling?" Sitting closer now, his eyes swept over her face seeing more bruising blossoming around her temple.

"Well, I'm okay right now because of drugs. Let's make sure they give me some of this to take home, okay?" Luke let out a laugh and looked down at her hand, there was still a bit of dried blood around her fingernails. He sobered instantly, full of emotion.

"Where's Kate?"

Luke cleared his throat. "She and the other girls are being monitored, but apparently they're all okay. They were just heavily drugged. Our neighbor, Jennifer, she put up a real fight, got a few scratches and cuts but nothing serious. I overheard the nurses talking to the cops, and it looks like it was her blood on that shirt we found. There were all these scratches on Phil's chest from the fight. Other than that, she and the rest of the girls aren't physically hurt; mentally, they'll all need therapy but...you're a hero."

She lightly picked up his battered hand and brought it to her lips, planting a small kiss on it. "I'm their hero, and you're mine. Thank you for coming."

"Did I ever give you any reason to doubt I would? Holly, I..." He felt overwhelmed and ran his undamaged hand through his hair in frustration. His breath came out shaky. "You don't understand what it was like to wake up and see your spot empty and then to read this—" He stood up and took the folded-up post-it note out of his pocket. "I went crazy."

She looked pained, tears brimming her eyelids. "Luke, I didn't—"

He didn't let her continue. "Please let me finish." He unfolded the post-it, silently reading it again.

"I called the police and literally ran straight to the unit because the thought of you being alone, scared, with him... And then getting there and seeing you, Holly, if you hadn't said something I don't know if I would've stopped hitting him. I wanted to kill him. I would want to kill anyone who would do this to you. Seeing you like this I—" His voice cracked, and he stopped, dropping his head, evening his breath out. "It kills me that I didn't get there sooner, that I couldn't stop him sooner, that I couldn't keep you safe."

He took a moment to compose himself and then met her eyes. "I want to keep you safe, to be with you, to make you happy all the time, to make sure you never dance alone." He grinned. "I've never met someone else who brings this out in me, but I guess I've never been in love before."

Her eyes widened, and tears spilled down her cheeks. "You love me?"

"I love you. I'm absolutely crazy in love with you, and I'm annoyed with myself for having taken so long to say it to you."

She giggled, wincing slightly as she jarred her ribcage. "I love you, too. I've wanted to tell you that for so long, but I've been scared."

When he stood and moved to the window, she asked, "What are you doing?"

Luke came back to her side, smiling broadly. "I'm about to kiss you, so I wanted to make sure I wasn't caught by that nurse." He cradled her face, careful not to apply pressure to her injuries, and planted a soft kiss on her lips. "After I nurse you back to health, I'm going to give you a proper 'I love you' kiss."

She raised an eyebrow, a dazed, dreamy smile gracing her lips. "What exactly is a proper 'I love you' kiss?"

Luke grinned. "One that ends with us in a bedroom for an entire night."

The two of them smiled like idiots at each other

when a knock on the door broke them out of their stupor. Officers Martinez and Shane entered the room.

Ben Martinez spoke first. "Evening, Miss Harrison, Mr. Morris. How are you two feeling?"

Holly winced as she attempted to sit a little straighter. Luke put a protective hand on her back, helping her balance as she spoke. "It's not the worst I've ever felt. But hey, you should see the other guy, right? That was mostly me."

Luke looked at the officers, who were trying to remain professional and not laugh. He explained in an amused voice, "She's on a lot of pain meds right now."

Both officers tried to maintain straight faces, but both were having a hard time hiding their shared amusement. "We actually just came from speaking with *the other guy*," Martinez replied. "You really did a number on him but nothing he won't recover from." He gestured to Luke's hand.

Holly chimed in. "Did he have a broken nose because I did that with this guy right here." She held up her arm, proudly brandishing her elbow while flinching at the sudden movement.

Officer Shane spoke up, his normal stern demeanor breaking down. "He did indeed have a broken nose. He will have plenty of time to nurse his wounds in jail though. All the victims are alive and stable, and I'm sure they'll all have plenty to say when they feel up for it. We've got enough evidence on him now to put him away for a long time. It's all thanks to you guys."

Luke shook his head. "It was all her, I was just the bodyguard."

Holly giggled. "I saved the day." Luke snorted with laughter, and her face went from happy to angry.

"Don't you laugh at me. I'm drugged, I'm in love"
—she turned to the officers—"I'm in love with him by
the way."

The officers visibly shook with laughter. "We're
going to leave you guys alone now. We'll be in touch."
They exited the room as Holly started to softly sing
something about hearing it for the boys.

Luke silently cursed himself for not having anything
to document this moment.

****

Later that same day, he went back and helped Kate
get home who, aside from being shaken, was cleared to
leave the hospital. After dropping her off, he left her and
Holly alone for the day as there were a lot of tears and
hugs happening upon the reunion. Soon after that,
Holly's friend Allie drove down from Wisconsin and
stayed with them to help out.

Luke just shook his head after she looked at him,
eyes narrowed. "I'm going to read your cards later
tonight."

Not knowing what that meant, he retreated to his
own place for the rest of her stay. After she left, Luke
and Kate took turns making sure Holly did not overexert
herself. By the end of the week, apart from her ribs, she
was almost back to normal.

"You're lying. I did not start singing." Holly
laughed as she and Luke sat on the back porch, enjoying
the warm weather and a cup of coffee. She was gently
holding his injured hand across the table, stroking the
skin that was visible above the bandages.

"You did, and I was so mad I didn't record it. You
felt a song in your heart and just had to let it out." Luke
smiled.

The swelling had gone down on her face, and the bruises had transformed from purple to yellow. Holly threw her hair back into a bun, displaying them proudly. Luke would be happy when they were gone for good, he did not want a constant reminder of the pain she went through.

Holly turned her head, smiling. "You know me, when I feel something, I just gotta say it. Speaking of which…" She turned and grabbed something out of her pocket. "I already okayed it with Kate in case you were wondering but um, I love you and I just want…um…" She looked down at her hand, a sheepish expression on her face.

Luke felt his stomach muscles tightening in anticipation.

"I've never given someone…um…ok, wow this sounded so much better in my head." She blew out a frustrated sigh and slapped her hand down on the patio table with a metallic clang and quickly pulled back, revealing a key. Luke looked at it and up at her. "I want you to have a key to my place so you can come over whenever you want and, even though you live across the hall, I've created space in my dresser for you to keep stuff in, and I love you so…yeah." Holly put her head in her hands and chuckled. "I wish I could say it's the concussion making me mess this up, but I'm just not very eloquent."

He stood up and grabbed her hand, gently pulling her up and circling his arms around her waist.

"I would love to accept a key to your apartment and give you one to mine. I can't wait to start using it, especially when you're ready to uh…participate in physical activities again." He raised his eyebrow, giving her a wicked grin. Holly stood up on tip toe, leaning into whisper.

"I can't wait."

Luke bent down and kissed her, and felt like he would never be alone again.

Epilogue

MURDER FOR YOUR THOUGHTS EXCLUSIVE

A few weeks back I, your friendly neighborhood murder blogger, wrote about a string of kidnappings that occurred in Chicago. Five ladies in total went missing, all different ages, all different ethnicities, all within the same neighborhood. I even updated you all when the fourth lady went missing, but now I get to do something I don't normally do.

I get to report on how this was all solved.

Apparently, people read this (take that, Mom.) and are fans of true crime, just like me. Apparently, they call themselves Murder-Heads (creepy but I love it, guys). One of those fans is named Holly Harrison and not only happens to live in the same neighborhood as the kidnappings but happened to be the one to find them all.

This amazingly badass lady lived in the building next to the man we now know as Phil Senter, the monster responsible for the kidnappings. Being the ever-vigilant woman, Holly reportedly saw Phil acting suspicious and reported him. Since I am incredibly charming, I was able to get an interview with the hero:

In her own words;

HH: "I saw him fondling a scarf, I immediately knew that he was someone who needed to be checked in on by the police."

When the checkup occurred and nothing came of it,

Holly kept watch, trusting her gut, knowing something was wrong here.

HH: "I'm not allowed to say too many details while the trial is going on but basically, we, my boyfriend Luke and I, kept our eye on him. We found some damning evidence..."

LM: "I found the evidence."

(Did I mention I interviewed both Holly and Luke? It was very cute)

HH: "Well, okay, you found it, but I got it back."

I was confused at this and asked to elaborate, Holly looked at me and said very nonchalantly,

HH: "Oh my apartment got broken into and the evidence was stolen. But I got it back...um I'm not really allowed to say how though."

RJ: "Ha, well I can't wait to hear all the details when you are able to tell it but for now, I can live with the broad story. So your friend ended up being one of the abducted ladies?"

HH: "Yes, Phil was onto us at that point, he knew that we totally reported him, and we're sure that I was the intended victim, not my roommate."

LM: "It doesn't matter though because she found her and saved her and the rest of the girls. She is incredible."

(A little writer's note for you all; I obtained this interview via video call, and Holly blushed awfully hard at this compliment. Like I said, they are so stinking cute. Love me a good true crime couple.)

Obviously, there is a lot more to the story but, once the sentencing for Phil has been decided, I will be going back and writing THE FULL story, just for all you murder-heads. Now let's all give a shout out to the baddest bitch there is. Thanks, Holly.—R.J.

"Read it to me again," demanded a giggling Holly.

She and Luke lay in her bed, snuggled under the covers. Autumn had arrived in Chicago, and with it came strong winds and the need to be encased under a blanket. Luke's hand, holding his phone, was raised above his head while his other was wrapped around Holly whose head was lying on his bare chest. The only thing covering them was the thin jersey cotton sheet on her bed.

"I'm not reading you a true crime blog post again. It's too long," he said as he clicked out of the window and tossed his phone on the nightstand, bringing his attention back to Holly. She sighed contentedly and looked up at him.

"I can't believe we got to talk to RJ. I can't believe how cool she was. I just want to be her friend." Luke bent his neck and kissed the top of Holly's head.

"She probably wants to be your friend too, who wouldn't want to be your friend?"

She turned her head and buried it into his abdomen.

"I am pretty great, aren't I?"

Luke laughed. "Yes, you are, but right now we have more pressing matters. I can hear the trees blowing and knocking against the windows, I'm pretty sure I can feel a breeze coming through the cracks, I need to keep you warm." He began to lift the sheet and Holly smiled, hoping he would keep her warm for a long time to come.

A word about the author...

Emilie Barage is a Chicago native who loves true crime and romance. She received her masters in Classics and works in marketing, reserving her free time to dream up stories. She is currently working on her second novel.

CPSIA information can be obtained
at www.ICGtesting.com
Printed in the USA
BVHW041414110422
633959BV00015B/641